Drummers

# of Jericho

CAROLYN MEYER

GULLIVER BOOKS
HARCOURT BRACE & COMPANY
San Diego   New York   London

Requests for permission to make copies of any
part of the work should be mailed to:
Permissions Department,
Harcourt Brace & Company, 6277 Sea Harbor Drive,
Orlando, Florida 32887-6777.

Gulliver Books is a registered trademark of
Harcourt Brace & Company.

Library of Congress Cataloging-in-Publication Data
Meyer, Carolyn.
Drummers of Jericho/Carolyn Meyer.—1st ed.
p.   cm.
"Gulliver books."
Summary: A fourteen-year-old Jewish girl goes to live with her
father and stepmother in a small town and soon finds herself the
center of a civil rights battle when she objects to the high school
band marching in the formation of a cross.
ISBN 0-15-200441-6 ISBN 0-15-200190-5 (pbk.)
[1. Prejudices—Fiction.   2. Jews—United States—Fiction.
3. Friendship—Fiction.   4. Stepfamilies—Fiction.]   I. Title.
PZ7.M5685Dr   1995
[Fic]—dc20   94-36105

The text was set in Garamond #3.

Designed by Lisa Peters
First edition
A B C D E
A B C D E (pbk.)
Printed in Hong Kong

for Vered, of course

Drummers of Jericho

PART ONE

August

Unusual Meeting

THIS WAS ONE of the moments Billy Harper would remember later, when the trouble was over and most people had forgotten about it. Not that *he* would ever forget any of it. Nor would *she*—the girl who came crashing through the bushes that August morning, chasing after her dog.

The temperature was on its way to a hundred degrees for the fifth straight day with no end of the heat wave in sight, and Billy was mowing the Shoemakers' lawn. As usual, the lawn mower was so dull it wouldn't cut butter, so it was taking him twice as long as it should. Old Mrs. Shoemaker was probably spying on him from behind the kitchen curtain, complaining to Mr. Shoemaker that the Harper boy was too slow.

Dang, it was hot! Sweat trickled down his back under his T-shirt and dripped off his nose. Billy took off his glasses and wiped his face on his sleeve. He'd stopped for a swig of water from his old Boy Scout canteen when there was a sudden commotion in the tall shrubbery that separated the Shoemakers' backyard from the one next door. A rangy black dog with gray spots burst through the bushes chasing after Mrs. Shoemaker's huge white cat, Minnie, followed by a girl in ragged cutoffs and a droopy plaid flannel shirt.

"Grab him!" yelled the girl.

Billy dropped his canteen and lunged, managing to snag the dog by the scruff of his neck. Minnie cast them all a scornful look and minced off toward her perch on the porch railing.

"Thanks a lot," the girl said. "That cat comes over all the time and teases him. She just drives him wild. He must have escaped when I wasn't looking. Bad dog!" she said, shaking her finger but not sounding real angry.

The girl tried to drag the dog off by his scruff, but the dog still had his eye on the cat and stubbornly dug in his four big paws. Then she managed to gather him up in her arms. He was still a pup, all gangly legs and long, sweeping tail, but he looked almost as big as the girl.

"I'll bring him for you," Billy volunteered. They transferred the dog from her arms to Billy's, clumsily because the dog was wriggling and Billy was so much taller than the girl. *She can't be over five feet,* Billy thought, *if that.*

"His name's Tripper," she said.

"Hi, Tripper. I'm Billy."

The girl laughed. She had a low, throaty laugh, and Billy noticed her even, white teeth. That wasn't all he noticed: she had long, dark hair, smooth and shiny as black satin. Her creamy skin was still pale in the middle of summer; by now his sister, Brenda, and his girlfriend, Tanya, and all the other girls he knew had acquired golden tans. This girl had the thickest eyebrows he had ever seen, almost like fur. She wore glasses, little gold-rimmed ones that made her dark eyes, fringed with long lashes, look even larger and brighter.

Pretty wasn't the right word for her, Billy thought, comparing her to Tanya. Tanya was pretty, and this girl wasn't anything like Tanya. But *beautiful* didn't quite fit either. *Unusual,* maybe. He gave up looking for the right word. *She must be new in town,* Billy concluded. He would definitely have noticed a girl like this if she'd been around awhile.

She was telling him her name, but he was so busy staring at her he didn't catch it. It sounded foreign and kind of unusual. Like her. He'd ask her again later when his arms weren't full of dog.

He followed her out of the Shoemakers' back-yard to a yellow brick house next door with a high peaked roof and a front door painted bright blue. Every time he came to work in the Shoemakers' yard, he'd wondered about the people who lived in that house. The front yard was in bad shape, noth-ing but a big weed patch, sprouting tight clumps of nut grass and goosegrass with tall seed heads. The shrubbery was wildly overgrown.

"Have you lived here long?" Billy asked as the girl marched ahead of him, her shirt flapping. The backyard was in even worse condition than the front, Billy observed. And the girl must be roasting in that flannel shirt.

"Almost two weeks," she said. "I moved here from Denver, to live with my dad and stepmother and my two little brothers. They've been here about a year." She buckled the dog into a collar at the end of a long chain that was hooked around a tree by the Shoemakers' old wire fence. "Tripper's been here about ten days. Remember that huge storm we had? The water was running down the street as high as the curb, just like a river. My dad and I went out to look at it, and this poor, miserable puppy, about half-drowned and half-starved, suddenly appeared out of nowhere. Dad let me bring him inside, even though my stepmother, Ellen, said we have to get rid of him. We named him Tripper because he kept falling over his own paws on the wood floors."

"What is he?" Billy asked. The dog was straining at the end of his chain, anxious to play. The girl petted him, and he calmed down.

"Dad says Australian shepherd, because of the weird spots. I think it looks like camouflage, don't you? But his head is shaped like a Labrador retriever. And Ellen says he must have some chow in him somewhere, because of the spots on his tongue. Show Billy your tongue, Tripper."

The dog obligingly yawned. Sure enough, there were spots on his tongue. "So are you going to get to keep him?"

The girl shrugged. "Ellen put an ad in the paper, to see if somebody would claim him. So far nobody has. She says we can't keep him because Dad is allergic. But I promised I'd get him a doghouse so he won't be inside. He's my responsibility. I have to pay for his food and vet bills and all, with money I earn taking care of my little brothers. But I'm afraid they'll be grown-up before I earn enough to pay for a doghouse."

"I could help you build one," Billy heard

himself say. "Me and my dad finished our garage last summer. All you'd have to do is buy some plywood and shingles."

What am I getting myself into? Billy wondered. He didn't have the slightest idea how to go about building a doghouse, but at that moment it didn't matter. He wanted to get to know this girl, whatever her name was, and if building a doghouse was the way to do it—well, he'd figure it out.

"You would?" A light went on in her dark eyes. "That would be so cool! When do you think we could do it?"

Billy thought a minute. This was Wednesday, and he was leaving Sunday afternoon for band camp. All ninety-six members of the Jericho High School Marching Band would pile into school buses with their instruments and go out to Camp Murchison for five days of intense rehearsal to work on their fall marching routine. The week after that, school started. So, if he was going to build this girl a doghouse, he'd have to do it in the next couple of days.

"Tomorrow? Could you get the stuff we need by tomorrow?"

The girl smiled. That great smile! "Sure. I'll ask Ellen. Just tell me what to get, and we'll get it."

"Your dad has tools, right?" He realized he was

going to have to get practical now. "Saw, hammer, like that?"

The girl got an uh-oh look. "I don't know. My dad isn't what you'd call handy around the house. But I'll check with Ellen. Don't worry, it'll work out. I'll *make* it work out!" Suddenly she squatted down and hugged the puppy. "Hey, Tripper! You're gonna have a house!"

Billy looked at the unusual girl tousling the dog's ears. "Would you tell me your name again?"

"Pazit. P-A-Z-I-T. *pah-ZEET.*" She stood up and pulled a ballpoint out of her shirt pocket. "Here, do you have something to write on?"

He didn't. She didn't either. Then she grabbed his hand, turned it over, and printed PAZIT in the palm.

"OK?" she said, laughing up at him. "See you tomorrow!"

Reluctantly, Billy went back to finish the Shoemakers' lawn. Mrs. Shoemaker docked his wages—she paid him the same rate she'd paid his brother, Richie, five years ago, three dollars an hour—for taking such a long break, even when it was basically her cat's fault. And he knew that when he came back next Saturday after band camp, the Shoemakers' mower would still be dull. But for once he didn't care. He whistled all the way home, even

9

though it was Wednesday—church night, and his night to cook.

EVER SINCE BILLY'S mother had gone to work at the bank, the Harpers had stuck to a meal schedule: chicken parts on Monday, spaghetti and hamburger meat on Tuesday, franks and beans on Wednesday, and so on. All Billy had to do was open two large cans of beans and warm them up with a package of hot dogs and fix some kind of salad. His dad didn't cook, but every Thursday he went grocery shopping, bringing home the same basic things each week, plus whatever the special was for the weekend when Billy's mom took over the cooking. Sometimes the sameness got boring, but it was also easy to know what was happening from day to day.

For instance, Mondays his parents bowled, Tuesdays his parents went to Band Boosters, and Wednesdays they went to the Prayer and Praise group at Jericho Bible Temple while Billy and his sister, Brenda, attended Teen Disciples. Everybody Billy knew went to church on Wednesday night. Tanya's family belonged to Mission Hill Christian up by the country club; Twig Terwilliger and his girlfriend, Ashleigh, attended Full Gospel; but Shawn Stovall would be at Teen Disciples with Billy tonight unless he could worm out of it. Sundays were all right, Shawn said, but he was tired of Wednesday nights. So was Billy, but he could never skip. His folks were real strict about that.

"It's not a matter of choice," his dad said when Billy had tried to get out of it. "Going to church on Sunday and on Wednesday night is just like going to school. When you're an adult, living on your own and supporting yourself, you make your own choices. But long as you're living under my roof, I say you're going to church." End of argument.

Billy looked at the name printed on the palm of his hand, PAZIT, and wondered where she went to church. Tomorrow, when he went to build the doghouse, he'd ask her. And in case she hadn't already found a church home, maybe he'd invite her to his.

Doghouse

"WHO WAS THAT, Zeetie?" Ellen asked, emerging from her studio. Her hands were coated with drying clay.

"Billy. I don't know his last name, but he's coming tomorrow to help me build a doghouse for Tripper," Pazit reported, "so we have to get all the stuff ready today. Some wood and nails, I guess, and whatever else you need for a doghouse. Shingles, too, I think he said. And tools—do we have a saw, Ellen?"

"That kid is going to build a doghouse?" Ellen asked doubtfully. "Do you even know him? How did you meet him?"

"Next door." Ellen required an explanation for

everything. "He was mowing the grass for those old people with the enormous white cat that Tripper hates and Tripper escaped and ran over there and I had to climb over the fence and crawl through some bushes to get him and Billy caught him and we brought him home. He said he'd build a dog-house, if we get all the lumber and stuff."

Pazit's first choice would have been to wait for her father to get home from teaching summer school and ask him to take her to the lumberyard, since he was more sympathetic to the idea of the dog in the first place. But Gus was always tired when he came home. First he'd want to watch the five-thirty news with Ellen while Matt and Brian climbed all over him, and then it would be time for dinner, which Ellen didn't like to postpone because the little guys got hungry and crabby. By that time probably the lumberyard would be closed. Pazit decided to go for it now.

"Do you think," she coaxed, "you could take me to the lumberyard right now? I'll pay for it," she promised, although her bank account was zero and her credits for baby-sitting already pledged to reimburse her parents for dog food and the collar and chain. "If you could lend me the money now, I'll pay you back as soon as I can."

"Would you put that in writing, please?" Ellen sighed. "OK, we'll go. Just give me a minute to clean up. You get Brian and Matt. And you have a list of everything you need, right?"

"Not exactly."

" 'Not exactly'? So what is it you want me to buy?"

Pazit saw the doghouse, and ultimately the dog, slipping away from her if she didn't do something. "Billy said the man at the lumberyard would know," she said. Not exactly the truth, but she'd bet that's what he would have said if she'd remembered to ask him.

And that was pretty close to what *did* happen. The lumberyard had some ready-made doghouses that were way too expensive, but when she and Ellen showed the salesman the kind they wanted to build, he made up a bill of materials and figured it all out for them.

"There went another twenty-five dollars," Ellen grumbled as they drove home with a couple of sheets of plywood and a bundle of shingles stashed in the back of the station wagon. "On top of twenty-five pounds of dog food, a collar and leash, and a round of shots. What's this friend of yours going to charge us, Zeetie?"

"I think he's doing it for nothing," she said, although he hadn't said anything about that.

"Wow," Ellen said with a grin. "*Tripper* must have made quite an impression on him."

Pazit pretended not to get what Ellen really meant. "Well, Tripper's a very handsome dog, or will be when he grows up. He's charming, you've got to admit that. And he's obviously very intelligent."

"I wouldn't go *that* far," Ellen said. "He seems pretty dumb to me."

Pazit was beginning to breathe a little easier. Ellen had been so cooperative about buying the stuff for the doghouse that she *must* be intending to let Tripper stay. Otherwise, why would she have bothered?

The dog was one of the few good things that had happened in the past two and a half months since Pazit had come back to the States from Israel and started fighting with her mother all over again. Pazit and Ruth both thought that a year apart would have taught them to get along, that everything would be better; but it hadn't, and it wasn't. So, not even two months after her return, glad to be back with her friends in Denver but locked in an on-going battle at home, Pazit had impulsively insisted on moving to Jericho to live with her father. Besides, she missed her every-other-weekend (and sometimes more often) visits with him and Ellen and the little guys. Gus had invited her to come along when they moved to Jericho. She'd refused. But now she changed her mind, certain this would work.

"You can't just run away every time something doesn't go the way you want it to," Ruth had shouted during their last big argument. But Pazit was adamant. She promised first her mother, and later her father and Ellen, that she'd stay for a minimum of a school year.

PAZIT HAD BEEN in Jericho for thirteen days, since the end of July. So far, aside from the heat, which was bad compared to Denver, things were going pretty well. Jericho seemed like a nice town with funky old houses like the one Gus and Ellen had bought. The courthouse on the square looked like a giant sand castle surrounded by trees with thousands of tiny lights that came on at dusk. On Pazit's first night in Jericho her father and stepmother had hired a college student to stay with the little guys and took her to dinner at Mario's, a white-tablecloth-and-candlelight restaurant, to celebrate her arrival. Ellen and Gus raised their wine glasses and proposed a toast, "To happy days with our daughter," which made her feel very good, and Pazit raised her Sprite and responded, "To my parents and my new home." She was still so angry at her mother that she didn't feel even a twinge of guilt.

Her father seemed really happy to have her

here. Ellen worked at being a Good Stepmother. Ruth referred to Ellen, with her streaky brown hair twisted up and pinned in a loose, wispy bun, as "that old hippie," but Pazit got along all right with her. Brian and Matt, her brothers—half brothers, to be technically correct—ages four and six, followed her around adoringly. Pazit was crazy about "the little guys," as she called them. They were two of the reasons she'd wanted to come here to live.

Her father had moved to Jericho a year ago from Colorado Springs to teach political science at Jericho College, just at the time Pazit was leaving for Israel. Ellen was a potter, an artist who also had a knack for fixing up run-down old houses. This yellow brick monster had plenty of room for Ellen's studio and an attic hideaway where Gus had his study and where the guest room was. They gave Pazit the guest room, which had its own bathroom with a claw-footed bathtub.

The room itself was great, with its sharp angles and sloping ceilings. Pazit hadn't been so thrilled with the way it was furnished, however. First there was the bed, a hideous antique that squeaked and groaned like an animal in pain every time she rolled over at night. Ellen said it was a family heirloom and there was no place else to put it, but after a few days Pazit persuaded Ellen to store the curlicue-carved headboard and footboard and to allow her to put the mattress on the floor.

Next to go were the eyelet-embroidered white curtains. "I hate bright bedrooms," Pazit announced. "Bedrooms should be dark, like caves." So they'd bought black window blinds and black sheets and a purple-and-black comforter to replace Ellen's grandmother's handmade quilt. Now the room was dim on even the brightest day. Pazit knew that Ellen disliked it but went along with it as part of her Good Stepmother routine.

Pazit had tacked posters on the slanted ceiling, a scene of the beach at Tel Aviv and an artistic photograph of a flute with a red rose, given to her by her flute teacher in Denver. Next she covered the walls with snapshots. Some were of friends back in Denver, especially her oldest and best friend, Rachel. Others were of cousins in L.A. and New York, and her brother Ari at college. But most of the pictures were of kids from the kibbutz.

Her favorite picture, taken by her friend Tovah in an orange grove where they had been picking fruit, was of a hilariously grinning group with Pazit in its midst. It was hard to believe that that picture had only been taken last August when Pazit had just arrived in Israel to begin the most wonderful year of her life. The most wonderful part of the wonderful year, Leon, wasn't in this picture. The saddest thing was that Pazit had no picture of him at all, just the brass treble clef sign he had given her that she wore on a thong around her neck.

Pazit had wished that year would last forever, but her grades weren't good enough for renewal of her scholarship, and neither of her parents had the money to pay for another year. So she had come home. She still wore the key to her dorm room on the thong with the clef sign and the gold Star of David her mother gave her last year for her Bat Mitzvah. The key was supposed to have been turned in when she left, but she'd kept it as a souvenir. She'd cried all the way home on the plane back to Denver and back to arguments with Ruth about everything imaginable—starting with the fact, of course, that Pazit had screwed up her grades enough not to get a scholarship for another year. Her mother couldn't forgive her for that, and Pazit couldn't forgive herself.

Things weren't perfect in Jericho either. There was, for example, the problem of eating kosher.

"I don't know what to feed you, Zeetie," Ellen had said, making up a grocery list the day after she arrived. "You'll have to tell me what's OK and what isn't."

"Don't worry about it," she tried to reassure Ellen. "I don't eat pork, but other than that . . ."

Ruth had always kept kosher, although she did

so somewhat by her own rules. "It doesn't matter so much what you eat when you're away from home," her mother always said. "It's keeping clean at home that's important." Ruth ate shrimp and lobster when she went out to restaurants, but not at home, and never, under any circumstances, ham or other meat from a pig.

When Pazit had announced that she was going to live with her father, her mother had said, "You won't eat kosher there, you know. And that's not the only thing you'll miss!" But by then Ruth and Pazit had been constantly at each other's throats, and eating kosher or not seemed like the least important thing in the whole world.

She'd been wrong about that, Pazit was beginning to realize: it *did* matter.

Ellen, determined to do the right thing, had quit buying bacon for Gus's Sunday breakfasts, but sometimes she forgot and served milk and meat at the same meal and was surprised to find out about other forbidden foods. "Shellfish I know about," Ellen said, "but *catfish?*"

"It's a scavenger," Pazit explained. "They eat dirty things." Ellen tried to reason that catfish were farm-raised now, entirely different from bottom feeders in a river. "But it's their nature," she told Ellen and then gave up. How could you teach somebody who wasn't Jewish what *kashrut* was all about? The easy thing, she figured, was to stick with fruit and vegetables. Since that first night at Mario's, she had practically lived on salad. At least she could be sure what was in it.

That worried Ellen. "You're only fourteen," Ellen said. "Your body's still growing. I don't think you're getting enough protein." Then Ellen proceeded to cook up a big pot of chicken soup because she must have heard all those stories about Jewish mothers and their chicken soup.

The weather was much too hot for soup, but Pazit had pretended it was what she'd been yearning for all along. And it was pretty good, if not exactly how Ruth made it.

The next major hurdle, after the white curtains and antique bed, was persuading Ellen to let Tripper stay, even temporarily, after he wandered in during the storm. But Gus argued, "It will be good for Pazit, it'll give her some responsibility and companionship, help her transition into the family." Of course the little guys loved the idea of having a puppy, and that may have been what saved him.

But then Tripper dug up some of Ellen's shrubs and munched on the petunias or whatever those flowers were that Ellen had so carefully planted in the backyard, and it was crisis time.

"He gnawed off most of the nandina I just put in," Ellen said, her voice trembling. "I want you to come out with me and look at this, Zeetie. You, too, Gus. That dog stripped off all the leaves and chewed the bush right down to the ground."

So she had followed her stepmother into the backyard to survey the latest damage, ready to apologize, to say whatever was needed to soothe Ellen. "I'll buy you some new ones, I really will," Pazit began, although it was not clear when she was going to earn enough baby-sitting credits to support the dog's destructive habits, or even his non-destructive ones, like eating.

Gus promised he'd solve the problem by fencing in a large area for Tripper's exclusive use, as soon as summer school was over, which would not be for another week, and before the fall term began. In the meantime, Tripper would have to be chained to a tree, free only when Pazit took him up to her room to spend the night. "Only temporarily," Ellen admonished. "Don't let him get the idea that he's a house dog." It was nearly too late already.

Tripper hated being chained up; he whined and carried on whenever Pazit left him alone. He dug a secret tunnel under the old fence that separated their backyard from the one next door and figured out a way to wriggle out of his collar when the cat teased him. Pazit had scratches all over her arms and legs from scrambling over the fence and diving through the bushes after him. But that did show what a smart dog he was.

Aside from these practical problems, things were looking fairly good. Rachel had written her a long letter and called four or five times, which, the girls knew, would stop the minute Rachel's mother saw the phone bill. A couple of kids had sent cards. Gus and Ellen were going out of their way to be nice. She had two little brothers who thought she was the greatest thing in the whole world. She had Tripper. Until today she hadn't met any kids her own age in Jericho, but now that had changed.

The worst thing, the thing that couldn't be changed, was not being with Leon. She knew without checking the calendar that it had been seventy-five days since she'd seen him. She longed to hear from him, but that was a problem, too: Leon spoke Russian and no English and they'd communicated mostly in Hebrew, which both were learning to speak but neither could write well. He'd called her once right after she got back to Denver, a frustrating exchange of mostly misunderstood phrases, except when Leon said, *"Ya tibya lublyu"*—"I love you," in Russian. He had promised to send a picture, but so far it hadn't arrived.

That night in her room, with Tripper curled up beside her, Pazit began a letter to Leon, partly in Hebrew and partly in English, struggling to tell him about the doghouse Tripper was going to have but nothing about the boy who was going to build it. She wanted to remind him she had not forgotten her promise to come back to Israel, but she didn't know how to say it well enough and anyway, as soon as she was back in the U.S., she realized how hard it would be to keep that promise. This made her sad and achy. It was such a stupid letter anyhow, such a poor statement of how she felt, that she crumpled it up and tossed it.

Next she wrote to her best friend.

Dear Rachel,

You would love the guy I met today—tall and really good-looking with curly blond hair, blue eyes, wire-rimmed glasses that don't look nerdish, and a great smile. His name is Billy and he's going to build me a doghouse! Well, not actually for me, but for Tripper.

That was the kind of news Rachel would like, but writing it made Pazit feel disloyal to Leon. She tossed that letter, too.

Then she started a letter to her mother, the first since her arrival in Jericho.

Dear Mom,

I've got a dog, black with gray spots, and it looks as though I'm going to get to keep him. I've met a boy named Billy and he's going to build Tripper a doghouse tomorrow.

But then Pazit was struck by such a confused rush of missing her mother mingled with anger at her that she couldn't write another word, and wept.

Carpenter

"TELL ME AGAIN," Billy said.

"*Pazit* is Hebrew. My last name is spelled T-R-U-J-I-L-L-O. Pronounced *troo-HEE-yo*. Trujillo is Spanish. The *J* sounds like an *H* and the double *L* is like a *Y*. Here," she said, "I'll write it down for you."

Billy watched her print her whole name in square letters right on the sketch of the doghouse layout. She had on the same baggy plaid shirt she wore yesterday, or one like it. Her glasses slid down her nose, and she pushed them up with her finger.

"I know this sounds stupid," Billy said, "but how did you get a name like that?"

"Same place you got yours. From my parents."

"But it sounds so . . . foreign."

"My mother's family is from Israel. She was born there, and she wanted me to have a Hebrew name. My brother Ari—also a Hebrew name—is from my mom's first marriage. He goes to college in Canada. My dad is Mexican American, born in Chicago. 'A Chicano from Chicago,' he likes to say. They met in Florida, got married in New York, and I was born in Denver. Then they got divorced, and my dad married Ellen, who is from San Francisco. He and Ellen had two kids and moved here. And now I'm here, too. My mom's still in Denver. So what's your story?"

Billy had been trying to concentrate on the sheets of plywood laid out on the ground, but he wasn't doing well. This girl kept getting him rattled. He put down his square and looked at her. "I was born right here in Jericho. So was my brother, Richie, and my sister, Brenda. So were my mother and father. And my grandparents on the Harper side. They always tease my mother about being an outsider, because her people live sixty miles west of here in Manasseh. They've been there all their lives. I've never been to New York or Chicago or San Francisco. I've only been out of the state twice, at church youth meetings in New Mexico. It was up in the mountains. I thought it was real pretty there. My big dream is to see the world. My dad says once I've seen it I'll be more than glad to settle down again in Jericho."

Billy was surprised he had told her all this. He didn't usually talk about his family, probably because all his friends were pretty much like him and had known him for a long time, so there wasn't a lot to tell. Shawn Stovall had been his best friend since their mothers took them to the Sunday school nursery as babies, and Billy had known Clay Terwilliger since kindergarten, long before anybody called him Twig. He'd met Tanya in middle school, when he was in seventh grade and she was in sixth, but they had been officially going together only since last year. Tanya had already started talking about their anniversary coming up in September. Tanya kept track of stuff like that in some kind of a scrapbook, like it was real important, which it was to her. It made Billy kind of uneasy, though. Pasting things in a scrapbook made everything that ever happened seem permanent.

Billy liked Tanya well enough. She was sweet most of the time and real pretty, too, with long blond hair that she flipped back over her shoulders and then let drift forward over her face so she could flip it back again. He loved to watch her do that. And her blue eyes! They were beautiful, there was just no other way to say it. Of course she knew it and that was why she always put on makeup to make her eyelashes look longer, no matter where she was going.

Billy glanced at the girl who had printed her name on the sketch of the doghouse: PAZIT TRUJILLO. He couldn't imagine Tanya wearing glasses like Pazit's.

"Look, do me a favor and check these measurements, OK?" he said, snapping back to the job ahead of him. "Just to make sure we've got everything right. And show me where to plug in the extension cord for the saw. Then we're ready to start cutting."

Billy had measured and drawn the outlines of each part of the doghouse—two each for the roof and sides, and one each for the floor, front, and back, seven pieces total—on the plywood with a thick carpenter's pencil. His dad had loaned him the pencil this morning and had given him a twenty minute lecture before he left for work on the general subjects of safety, responsibility, and doing the job right. "A good carpenter measures twice and cuts once," he'd said. Billy had measured about five times now, and he still wasn't sure if he had allowed enough for the overlapping joints.

Billy clamped a sheet of plywood to the picnic table and checked the saw that belonged to Pazit's stepmother. Just as he turned it on, the back door flew open and two little kids dashed out, their mother right behind them. Billy shut off the saw. "Ma'am," he said, "if you don't mind, I'd appreciate it if you'd keep the children inside. Just in case of flying debris."

The lady gave him a warm, friendly grin. "Of course. You're Billy, right?" She stuck out her hand. "I'm Ellen Scanlon, mother of these two scamps."

Scanlon? Not Mrs. Trujillo? His mom always made fun of women who didn't use their husband's name. "Women's libbers," she called them. Billy wondered if he should call her *Ms.*

"I'm also the wicked stepmother of your assistant here," said Ellen Scanlon. "Right, Zeetie?"

"Right." But she gave Billy a funny look, one thick black eyebrow arched.

"Let me know when you're ready for a Coke or a Sprite. And I've got the makings for sandwiches. Whatever you'd like, just let me know, OK?"

After the lady and her two kids were safely out of the way, Billy turned on the saw again. The whirling blade bit into the plywood with a satisfying whine. Tripper watched uneasily from the tree where he was chained and howled at the screech of the saw. As Billy finished cutting each piece, Pazit took it away and laid it out on the grass.

Billy showed her how to butt the sections and

glue the joints. Then he gave her a lesson in drilling holes for the screws. "See, first you mark where you want it to go, then you punch a pilot hole with a nail. Then you drill. But you have to be sure to use the right size bit."

He made her examine the screws they were going to use until she'd figured out the right bit for the drill. He discovered that he enjoyed teaching Pazit the techniques of carpentry, the way his dad had taught him.

Pazit practically grabbed the drill out of his hand and, after a few rounds of practice on some scraps, began to screw the sides and back to the floor of the doghouse. She didn't have much patience, Billy thought. His dad would have had something to say to her about that.

The work progressed pretty smoothly, except when Billy switched to a jigsaw to cut the arched entryway in the front. It came out a little bit crooked, and when he tried to correct it, it turned out even worse.

"Hey, I'm sorry," he said. "It doesn't look so good, and there's not enough plywood to cut a new front."

Pazit shrugged. "You think Tripper is really going to *care*? I don't." And that ended that. She started drilling holes to attach the front.

Billy was enjoying himself. He liked the smell

of the raw wood and the whine of the saw and the powdery feel of the sawdust and the pleasure of seeing something taking shape. He tried to imagine building a doghouse with Tanya and failed. He could hardly wait to tell his dad about how well this was turning out. It was going to be a good doghouse, for sure.

He began to think how he was going to brag to Tanya about the doghouse, but then he wasn't sure exactly how he'd go about doing that. Somewhere in Billy's story he'd have to tell her about Pazit and how he'd met her. Then she'd want to know how much he had gotten paid for doing it, and she wouldn't like that he had done it for free.

Billy would see Tanya the next night. Friday nights except during football season and most Saturday nights they did something together, sometimes with Twig and his girlfriend, Ashleigh. He had plenty of time to figure out what to say.

All that was left to do was the roof. Billy's idea was to hinge it, so that the doghouse could be opened from the top in order to clean it out. But he was still trying to figure out how to do that when Pazit's stepmother came out with a tray of food.

"Feel free to go inside and wash up first, Billy," she said.

Billy was glad to. For one thing, he was curious

about the inside of the house with the blue door. Pazit led the way into the kitchen where kids' drawings were taped all over the refrigerator and lower cupboards. "Bathroom's there," she said, pointing to a door with a hand-lettered sign on it that said Men and Women.

When Billy came out, nobody was around. He could see them all in the backyard. Mrs. Trujillo, or whatever she called herself, was making a sandwich, Pazit was playing with Tripper, and the two little boys were examining the roofless doghouse, trying to climb inside. Billy stepped cautiously down the hall toward the front door and peered into the living room. This sure wasn't like his house. His mom liked things to match, and nothing here matched. Big, oddly shaped pots stood along the walls and on the table in front of a sofa that was draped with some kind of Indian rug. The table itself was made out of pieces of scrap metal with a glass top. A woven thing with bits of wood hung on the wall above the fireplace. Billy wanted to investigate further, but he knew this wasn't polite. Snooping, his mother would call it, although he bet she'd snoop, too, in a place like this. He went back outside.

"Help yourself," Pazit said, munching a sandwich with a big leaf of lettuce sticking out. Billy hated lettuce. He looked for bologna or some kind of lunchmeat, but there wasn't much but rabbit food and cheese. He went for the cheese. And there was no white bread—only the dark, grainy kind.

"Can I get you something else?" Mrs. Trujillo asked. "Since Zeetie came here, we've not been eating much meat."

"No, ma'am, this is fine," he lied. "Thank you." He'd fix himself a real sandwich when he got home.

He didn't feel that hungry now anyway. He wasn't used to eating with strangers, even though Mrs. Trujillo was trying hard to make him feel welcome and comfortable. She was asking him a lot of questions about himself, how old he was, what year he was in school, if he had brothers and sisters, what part of town he lived in, things like that, but if he had a mouth full of bread and cheese he couldn't answer.

"Fifteen, but I'll be sixteen in November," he responded. "I'm a junior. My brother, Richie, goes to Tech, and my sister, Brenda, is a senior at Jericho High. I live about a mile north of here, near the bypass on Pennsylvania. Just like the President."

Pazit didn't say much. She just watched him and nibbled around and around her cheese-and-lettuce sandwich. "Tell us about the high school, Billy," said Pazit's stepmother.

"I don't know what to tell you, ma'am, except

it's a great place. The best thing is the band. We win prizes at all the big competitions. We're the best in the region," he said proudly. "And near tops in the state, too, even among the big high schools."

"Are you in the band, Billy?"

"Yes, ma'am. I'm a bass drummer."

"I intend to play in the band," Pazit said. "I play flute."

"You do? Hey, that's great!" This was good news. Billy could imagine how much fun it would be to have this girl in the band. "So you're going to band camp next week, right?"

She shrugged and reached for a another piece of lettuce, which she rolled up like a cigar and bit daintily. "I didn't know about band camp. I haven't even registered for school yet."

"Mr. Dalrymple won't let you play if you haven't been to band camp. The Colonel's real strict about that."

"I bet he'll let me. I'm a good flutist. I was in a marching band in middle school, and I can memorize really fast."

Billy didn't say anything. He didn't question that Pazit was a good flute player or that she had marching experience. But he doubted that Mr. Dalrymple—everybody called him "the Colonel" behind his back—was going to change any rules.

After lunch Billy figured out how to put the

35

hinges on the doghouse roof. When that was finished, although he had never done it before, he and Pazit nailed on rows and rows of shingles.

"Now," Pazit announced, "we shall paint."

He couldn't believe the color she wanted to paint the doghouse: the same bright blue as the front door. "I've never seen a blue doghouse before," Billy said. "You sure that's what you want?"

"I'm sure. Anyway, we have the paint, and it's silly to buy more when we've got this. Here, I even found two brushes."

So they painted the doghouse blue.

They finished just as Pazit's father got home from teaching summer school, driving up in an ancient VW bug. Pazit introduced him. Billy thought she did it well, but he guessed that someone who had traveled as much as she had would know how to do things like that. Billy hated trying to introduce people. He never could remember whose name to say first.

"Look, Dad," Pazit said, showing him how the roof opened up.

"You could paint designs on the ceiling," her dad said, his arm across Pazit's shoulders. "Like the Sistine Chapel. Little doggie cherubs with wings and halos. Tripper would go wild over that, I'm sure." He stroked her hair, fondly. "Listen, *mi hijita,* I'm going inside to watch the news. You're welcome to join us, Billy," he added. "It's one of the high points of my day, especially after I've taught for four hours."

"Thank you, sir," Billy said. "But if it's that late I've got to get home."

He remembered the rest of his dad's lecture this morning: clean up your mess; put away your tools. Pazit helped.

"What did your dad call you?" Billy asked.

"*Mi hijita*. It's Spanish for little daughter. He's always called me that."

"Your stepmother calls you something else. Zeetie."

"Yes, and I don't like it, but the little guys started it and then she picked it up."

"OK, so I guess I won't call you Zeetie."

"And I won't call you William."

"Are you going to paint pictures on the ceiling?" he asked.

She laughed. "He was just joking around, as usual. I think it's perfect the way it is. Tripper thanks you, and I thank you."

He wished she would say something like "When are you coming back?" But she didn't, and he couldn't think what to say either. "See ya," he said, and she nodded and said, "See ya." He got on his bicycle and rode off.

Halfway home he thought of the Trujillos'

ragged front yard. He should have offered to mow it. Maybe they'd ask him to trim the shrubbery, too. Too late to go back now, he decided; it would look like he thought they owed him a job. He'd have to wait until he went to do the Shoemakers' when he got back from band camp and hope he'd run into Pazit again. It seemed like a long time to wait.

Counting the Days

PAZIT AND GUS moved the doghouse close to the tree where Tripper was chained. Ellen came out with an artist's brush and a small jar of black paint and lettered TRIPPER above the slightly crooked entryway in graceful script. The little guys insisted on putting their names on the doghouse, too, so Pazit helped them paint BRIAN and MATT on the back where no one would see it but they'd know it was there.

On Saturday Gus bought Tripper a fancy dog dish and a rawhide bone and proposed that they have a doghousewarming, which was just his excuse to barbecue in the backyard. While she helped to carry out the plates and utensils, Pazit found herself wishing Billy was there.

This was really stupid, all this thinking about Billy. She hardly knew him! As she set the table, her mind veered to Leon in Israel. It was now seventy-eight days and still no picture, although if it arrived in Denver after she left, no telling what her mother might have done with it.

She had tried to tell Ellen about Leon, to explain why she had been haunting the mailbox. "He's from Russia," Pazit told her, "and he's a student at the conservatory in Jerusalem where I used to go for flute lessons. He plays cello."

"Mmmm, sounds interesting. How old is he?"

Pazit started to fudge a little, but then she decided to be honest. It couldn't make that much difference to Ellen anyway. "Twenty-five," she said.

"Twenty-*five!*" Ellen had rolled her eyes. "A little old for you, I'd say." That annoyed Pazit, because it was so unfair.

"That's not so much," she argued. "I know lots of people where the husband is ten or even twenty years older than the wife. Dad's older than you, isn't he?"

"Eight years. But the older you get, the less

difference it makes. Eleven years is a lot of difference when you're only fourteen, even a very mature young woman like you. At Leon's age, he's more likely to have, uh, different expectations than a boy closer to your own age."

"I suppose you mean someone like Billy," Pazit said sarcastically to Ellen.

"I wasn't even thinking about Billy, but yes, now that you mention it."

The thing about Billy was that he was a year and a half older than her and really nice, but he was a *kid.* If you were used to older boys, to *men,* then somebody like Billy was bound to seem even more like a kid, especially since boys mature more slowly than girls. Pazit had a theory: boys like Billy could be friends, even good friends, almost the way girls were friends, but you couldn't feel the same way about them as you could about a man like Leon. *That* was something totally different.

ELLEN'S REACTION was a disappointment— Pazit expected the "old hippie" to be more broad-minded—but it was mild compared to what her mother's had been. This had been one of their worst fights. Ruth had come completely unglued when she'd wormed a partial truth out of Pazit: that Leon was older. Pazit had admitted that he was "around

41

twenty-one," which sounded less alarming than twenty-five and wasn't so far off to be an outright lie.

"You don't trust me!" Pazit had cried while Ruth raved.

"It's not *you* I don't trust, it's *him*," Ruth yelled back. "A twenty-one-year-old man has only one thing on his mind when he's with a fourteen-year-old girl." Later, when the fight had run out of energy and they had cooled down, Ruth had taken a different approach. "My worry is that you look so much older than your age." she said. "People think you're eighteen, nineteen, even twenty. Did you tell Leon that you are only fourteen?"

"He knew that. It didn't matter to him."

Actually Pazit hadn't told him anything at all. When he asked her age, she told him to guess, and he'd guessed twenty, and she hadn't corrected him. She liked the idea of looking older, of people thinking she was an adult.

"I was the same as you," Ruth continued. "When I was your age, all the young men thought I was much older. I liked it, too. But now I believe it's not so good. So. Write to this Leon and tell him you are only fourteen, and if he wants to continue being a friend, that's fine, but that's as far as it will go."

Of course Pazit hadn't written the letter. She

didn't know how to explain it in Hebrew anyway, and she would not ask Ruth for help.

WEARING A LONG white apron that had *El Jefe*—"the chief"—lettered across the front in red, Gus lined up a row of hamburgers on the grill. Ellen wrapped ears of corn from the farmers' market in foil. Pazit made a tuna sandwich to go with the salad she'd fixed. Gus brandished his spatula and announced, "In honor of the doghousewarming, I've hired a fence company to come and build a dog run for Tripper, since I don't have time to do it, and to be perfectly honest, the talent or the desire."

It was settled, then. Tripper was staying, an official member of the family. Pazit gave everyone a hug, including, of course, Tripper, and Matt and Brian fed him half their burgers.

SEVENTY-NINE DAYS since she'd left Israel for Denver, seventeen days since she'd left Denver for Jericho . . . On Sunday Pazit stayed in her darkened room, writing letters and listening to music. For weeks after she'd come home from Israel she had listened to nothing but a tape of brooding Russian music that Leon had given her, playing it over and over. But since she'd moved to Jericho she'd gone back to albums of flute music by Jean-Pierre Rampal and James Galway, and sometimes she put on Zamfir and his panpipes and made up dances to go with the haunting music. And she had her collection of grunge and rap, which she cranked up to full volume.

On Sunday afternoon just before five o'clock, Pazit turned down the music, left her bedroom door ajar, and listened for the phone. Ruth had gotten into the habit of calling on Sundays about this time. Maybe, Pazit thought, her mother picked that time because she was thinking about the Sunday suppers they used to have together. Before Pazit went to Israel and again before she moved to Jericho, Pazit and her mother had a weekly ritual of going out to a vegetarian restaurant, just the two of them, even if they had had a huge argument an hour before that had ended with slammed doors.

Before the big fight about Leon, they had mostly fought about Pazit's grades, which were generally pretty bad. Unlike her brother Ari the Brain who excelled at everything academic, Pazit didn't care much about school—at least not the academic side of it. She enjoyed the social part, hanging out with her friends. Some of her teachers had been OK, but most of them were truly awful, in Pazit's opinion, and unbelievably boring.

There was always that "You're not living up to your potential" trip being laid on Pazit and the inevitable comparisons with Ari. Her mother had worked hard to make sure Pazit was assigned to accelerated classes, the kind Ari had skimmed through with top grades, but Pazit always managed to do so poorly that the teachers would insist she be transferred out. That would make Ruth furious—at Pazit and at the teachers.

Then the fighting would begin. "You want me to be somebody else!" Pazit would yell. "I want to be myself!"

"I just want you to be the best Pazit you can be," Ruth would argue, but Pazit didn't buy that. Not really. Her mother wanted her to be like Ari.

Ari was a talented oboist. The scholarships he won had been in music as well as in math and science. "See why it's so important for you to keep up your flute?" her mother had admonished. "If Ari can do it . . ."

" 'If Ari can do it,' " Pazit mocked.

What they never discussed was that Ari's social skills were zip, whereas Pazit's were good-to-excellent. She could make friends anywhere. She had left dozens in Denver, gathered dozens more in Israel. And that wasn't even counting the boys—*men*—who got big crushes on her. Men like Leon, who would someday be the next Rostropovich, internationally renowned as a cellist.

After Ari had gone away to college, Pazit thought her life would be better with her

45

accomplished brother out of the house, but she'd been wrong. With Ari gone, it was like being an only child, with all of Ruth's energy totally focused on her. Ruth wanted Pazit to be the best at everything—the best flute player, the best figure skater, the best student. But the harder her mother pushed, the less well Pazit did, and the more they fought. The smallest disagreement often escalated into all-out warfare.

To make matters worse Pazit and her friend Rachel had gotten into trouble a couple of times. The girls had been best friends since they were little kids and attended the same Jewish Sunday school. They'd prepared for their Bat Mitzvahs together. They'd been in the same B'nai B'rith Youth chapter. One night they told their mothers they were going to sleep over at the house of another friend, but instead they'd taken off to an all-night party. When they were caught the first time, both were grounded for weeks. The next time something like that happened, more stringent measures were called for.

Their parents had decided to send the girls to Israel, where both families had relatives. They all knew people who had put their kids in an American school in Israel, and the kids had loved it and learned a lot and everybody had been happy. Pazit had gone willingly, partly because Rachel was going, too. And she *had* loved it. She and Rachel had gone on school trips to Haifa and Tel Aviv and on a long bus ride all the way to Egypt where they'd slept in a Bedouin tent. But when the money and the scholarship ran out at the end of the year, she'd returned home to Denver. Rachel's parents were divorcing, so she went home, too. They'd flown back on the same plane.

While Pazit was in Israel, Ruth had written long, loving letters about how much she missed her, but the minute Pazit came home, they fell into arguing again. Pazit had said some pretty ugly things to her mother, and that pained her. The year away hadn't changed anything between them.

"Fine," her mother had yelled after their last major fight, which was not about Ari or Leon but about something so minor Pazit couldn't even remember what it was, "go live with your father then, if I'm such a bad mother. You think it will be better with him and that old hippie? Go! You think with two little brats in the house it's going to be like *Leave It to the Bradys,* whatever that show is called? Go!" Ruth never could keep the old TV sitcoms straight. "But you will not come back to this house until you learn how to behave like a respectful daughter!"

Pazit had packed two suitcases and barely had time to call Rachel.

47

"I never even heard of Jericho!" Rachel wailed, although Pazit was sure she had told her about it before, when Gus and Ellen moved there. "How long are you going to stay?"

"Until the end of the school year," Pazit said. "That's what I promised all of them. After that I don't know what will happen."

"You'll never last," Rachel predicted. "You'll be back long before then."

Pazit and Ruth had been silent on the drive to the airport. Pazit was too angry and too hurt to trust herself to say anything. "You can just drop me off at the entrance," Pazit muttered. The last thing she wanted was another scene.

"No," her mother said firmly. "I want to see you get on that plane."

Ruth had waited with her until her flight boarded and reached out tentatively to hug her, but Pazit was in no mood to be touched. She'd turned away. Later she was sorry she had done that.

Pazit missed her mother in ways she would never have imagined. Ruth could walk into a clothing store and know exactly what to buy for her—size, color, style, everything—that's how well she knew her. And they had often gone ice skating together. Pazit loved to skate, and Ruth herself was a fantastic skater who'd had Pazit out on the ice when she was two and in figure skating classes by

48

the time she was four. Gus couldn't even stand up on skates, and even if he could, there was no ice rink anywhere near Jericho. The thought of her skates hanging in her closet back in Denver made Pazit homesick.

Ruth had called the first Sunday after Pazit arrived in Jericho. The conversation was brief: "Are you all right?" "I'm fine, Mom." "Good."

The call the following Sunday was about the same. Pazit had not even told her mother about the dog.

Now, the third Sunday, Pazit waited, looking forward to the call and dreading it at the same time. When the phone rang at ten after five, Pazit ran to pick it up.

"Hello, sweetheart, how are you?"

"Fine, Mom."

"That's good. When does school start?"

"Not for another week."

"Have you registered for classes?"

"Dad's taking me this week."

"He should have done it before now. You won't get in the good classes."

"I'll get in good classes, Mom. Don't worry."

"You're starting over completely. No one knows you or your brother. You'll probably be ahead of most of the students there. You should be an honor student. No more excuses."

49

"Right," Pazit said through clenched teeth.

"Now let me talk to your father. Love you, darling."

"Love you, Mom."

She laid down the phone and called her father and went back to her room. The only good thing about school she could think of was that she had one friend: Billy.

Mowing

THE DAY AFTER he came back from band camp, Billy rode his bike down to mow the Shoe-makers' lawn. His plan was that after he finished, he'd go next door and offer to do the Trujillos', too.

But there was Pazit's stepmother with a faded red bandanna tied around her hair, pushing a clunky old power mower back and forth across the front yard. As Billy rode up, the mower sputtered and quit. Billy swung off his bike and leaned it against a hackberry tree. She was yanking the starter cord, and nothing was happening. He walked close so she'd look up and notice him.

"Why, Billy!" Mrs. Trujillo said, straightening up. "Am I ever glad to see you! You know something about these machines, right?"

"Some," he told her. "I do yard work for a living. The Shoemakers are my customers."

Billy knelt on the rough weeds and examined the mower. It was dirty, covered with black gunk, and probably hadn't been sharpened in years, even worse than the Shoemakers'. But when he jerked the starter cord, the engine caught.

"There you go, ma'am," Billy said, stepping back from the snarling engine. "But I think you ought to take it in for a tune-up soon as you can."

"You are a miracle worker!" Mrs. Trujillo pulled off the bandanna and wiped her face and neck. "Would you consider taking on another client?" she asked with a smile. "If I promise to get the mower in shape for you?"

"Yes, ma'am," Billy said. "I generally get paid five dollars an hour." Not exactly true, but what the Shoemakers should be paying him.

"You've got yourself a deal," she said turning off the mower, and they shook hands. "I don't suppose you'd want to finish up what I've started today?"

"Yes, ma'am. I'll be back soon as I get done at the Shoemakers'."

Billy tried to rush through his mowing next

door, but Mrs. Shoemaker had an extra chore for him—digging up pecan seedlings that were sprouting all over her yard from nuts that had fallen from the Trujillos' tree next door. Armed with an ancient butcher knife, Billy dug while Mrs. Shoemaker, in a yellow housedress and bedroom slippers, hovered around him to make sure he pulled out the whole thing and didn't cheat and cut off the little tree at the soil line, leaving a long root ready to start over.

"You working for them folks?" she asked, indicating Pazit's house with her chin.

"Yes, ma'am," Billy said. "I'm fixin' to."

"Well, they need it. Seem mighty peculiar, don't they?"

"No, ma'am, I don't think so." He wrestled out another pecan and dropped it in a paper sack.

"Mr. Shoemaker kinda gets the idea they might be communists."

"Communists?" Billy tried not to laugh. Nobody worried about communists anymore, but maybe the Shoemakers were too old to quit. "Where'd you get that idea?"

"*She* come over here and introduced herself and the little boys when they moved in. Couldn't make out the name. *He* teaches at the college. Political science. And she's some kinda artist, I guess. He's *divorced,* you know that, and the girl is his. And we heard that the girl come from Israel, so she must be a Jew. Whole family might be Jews. You missed some over here," she said, jabbing a gnarled finger.

"But that doesn't make them communists."

"Lots of Jews are communists."

Billy knew better than to argue. These were old people, they went to his church, and he knew he should be respectful. *Just get done,* he told himself, prying up the seedlings he'd missed, *and go.*

As soon as he'd finished and collected his wages—Mrs. Shoemaker paid him a dollar extra for the pecan trees—Billy went next door. The mower was where he'd left it. He got it started again and nursed it along, thrashing through the stubborn weeds. He did the front yard and started in back, where Tripper barked amiably at him. Billy kept glancing toward the house, wondering if Pazit would see him and come out. But there was no sign of her.

When he was through, Billy pressed the door-bell and waited. The door jerked open. Pazit stood there dressed in jeans with ripped knees and a T-shirt with a yellow six-pointed star on the front. "I'm done with the yard," he said.

"Come on in," she said, stepping back. He was so glad to see her that he almost fell over the

54

threshold. One of her little brothers saw him and giggled. "Matt, go get Mom, OK?"

Billy waited uncomfortably. Fortunately, Mrs. Trujillo came right away. "You'll never know how much I appreciate this, Billy," she said, handing him two crumpled fives, more than she actually owed. "And I *promise* I'll do something about that mower before you come again."

"It would be good if you had an edger," he said, stuffing the bills in his pocket. "Then I could do nice neat edges along the walks and so on. It makes it look real professional."

"I'll think about it," Mrs. Trujillo said. "Thanks for the suggestion."

"Also," he added, "your shrubbery sure needs trimming, if you don't mind me saying so."

"All right," Mrs. Trujillo agreed. "Come back next week and you can do the whole thing. Why don't you stay and have a Coke, Billy?"

Pazit got them sodas and they went outside. While they sat under the patio umbrella, Pazit's dad came out to wash the cars, and the two little boys helped. A water fight broke out between Mr. Trujillo and the kids, who were hollering and screeching at the top of their lungs, getting the dog all wound up.

Billy studied Pazit's shirt with the star and a

bunch of symbols, like writing of some kind. When he finally asked about it, she explained that it was called a Mogen David, a Star of David, and the writing was Hebrew.

"It says, *Shalom aleichem,*" she explained. "It means 'peace be with you.' You say it like hello or good-bye. It's my BBYO shirt—B'nai B'rith Youth Organization. I belonged to a chapter in Denver."

He sipped his soda slowly. He could have sat there all day, listening to her talk about the strange things she knew that were completely foreign to him. But, as usual, he had to get home.

On the way home he stopped off at Ashleigh's Flowers, a florist shop owned by Twig's girlfriend Ashleigh Reynolds's parents, and bought his mother an African violet with part of his yard money. It was Mrs. Harper's birthday, and she loved houseplants. He set aside a dollar-forty for church—he had been taught to tithe, to give a tenth of everything he earned to the church—and put the little bit that was left in the "Car Jar" he kept under his bed. He was saving up for a car, once he got his license, but his car fund was still pitifully small.

Saturday evening his whole family—including Tanya; Brenda's boyfriend, Chuck Johnson, who was drum major of the band; Richie Junior, home from Tech for the weekend; and Richie's fiancée,

Lucinda—went to Red Lobster for the birthday dinner. They were all laughing and joking and having a good time, when out of nowhere a picture of Pazit appeared in Billy's head: her funny laugh and her torn jeans and the T-shirt with the Star of David and the Jewish writing on it.

When his mother's birthday cake—glittering with sparklers—was delivered to the table, and the waiters gathered around to sing, Billy was busy thinking about what he'd say to Pazit when he saw her next, and wondering what she'd say to him.

PART TWO

Jericho High School

Red Zone

THE FIRST DAY was a zoo. Billy felt sorry for the freshmen, coming into this big high school from their little middle schools all around Jericho. He remembered how nervous he had been when he was a freshman and everybody seemed to know what they were doing except him.

He kept looking for Pazit. She seemed like a girl who could take care of herself, after traveling to all those places and actually going to school in a foreign country. But still, it was bound to be hard, not knowing anybody.

Before his first class, Billy made a quick detour through the Red Zone, the hall where the freshmen had their red-painted lockers. He was looking for

Pazit, just to say hi and welcome, but Red was the zooiest place of all and he didn't see her.

He decided to check the area again before lunch. But it was his bad luck to finally get a glimpse of Pazit's satiny black hair just as Tanya caught up with him. "You going to lunch, Billy?" Tanya asked, and he said he was because there was no way out of it.

That made it definitely out of the question to go over and talk to Pazit. Tanya wouldn't have liked him showing any interest in another girl, but especially somebody like Pazit. Somebody unusual. So he didn't give any sign that he had even noticed her and hoped she hadn't noticed him either. Later he felt maybe he should have spoken to her anyway, Tanya or no Tanya.

Tanya held his hand while they walked to the cafeteria. Pazit walked several yards ahead of them. The first day of school, when everybody was trying to make a good impression, she was wearing floppy black pants that tied at the ankle and a lacy sweater with something bright pink under it that showed through the holes and an orange shawl draped around her hips. Long pants *and* a sweater *and* a shawl in this steaming heat, almost a hundred degrees!

He glanced down at Tanya, her fingers laced through his. She was dressed in her red-and-white

Junior Demonettes uniform, the short drill team outfit that showed off her long, tanned legs. She was allowed to wear it to school when they had pep rallies or on special occasions like the opening of school. When the girls pranced out on the gym floor or the football field and performed their precision routine, Billy always felt proud that one of them was his girlfriend.

Next year Tanya would be eligible for the senior drill team that performed at halftime. She worried all the time that she wouldn't make the regular Demonettes, and it seemed to be up to Billy to always tell her, "Sure you will, anybody pretty as you, and you're real good, too."

Some girls, like Tanya, were just naturally good-looking. Tanya dreamed about becoming a model and almost had her folks talked into sending her to modeling school. But some girls—and Billy felt sorry for them when Shawn Stovall pointed them out—you could tell would always be kind of homely no matter what they did to themselves. Now, Billy realized, there was a third category: the girls who made up their own rules. Sophisticated girls. So far he knew only one.

The first week of school the upperclass guys looked over the freshman girls, sizing them up. Seniors, naturally, were in the best position, like they were kings. When you were a freshman, the only girls you knew were from the middle school you'd gone to plus a few from your church. Pretty soon you got to know other girls, mostly ninth graders, from other middle schools around Jericho or maybe some other little town out in the country.

There was no way anybody would mistake Pazit Trujillo for a Jericho girl. Everything about her was different: the pale, creamy skin when everybody else had a tan, the sleek black hair, the dark eyes, even the little gold-rimmed glasses set her apart. He knew for a fact that Tanya was bat-blind, but she'd worn contact lenses practically since childhood; there was always some crisis with a lens getting lost or something. But Pazit's clothes, more than anything, were what made her stand out from everybody else.

Naturally the guys were checking her out but being cool about it, not letting on, because their girlfriends would probably kill them or something if they found out. Girls were like that, Billy knew from observing his sister and her friends, but naturally they were all checking out Pazit, too.

Billy looked again for Pazit in the band room fourth period, but she wasn't there. Probably the Colonel had told her she couldn't be in the band because she hadn't been to band camp, and Billy was sorry he'd been right about that. But as he and Twig and Shawn Stovall were leaving at the end of class, he spotted her waiting outside Mr. Dalrymple's office.

"Check out the immigrant," Shawn muttered. "Anybody know who she is?"

"Her name is Pizza True Jello," Twig said. "I was right behind her in the cafeteria line, and I saw it written on her notebook."

"Pizza True Jello!" Shawn had snickered. "Nobody's got a name like that. Who'd make their kid sound like a menu? You sure that's what it is?"

"Something pretty close," Twig insisted. "I think it might be Mexican. A real weird name. She looks kind of weird, too."

Billy opened his mouth to set them straight, and then he shut it again. At that moment a tug of war began inside Billy, pulling him one way and then the other. On the one hand, he wanted to go over to Pazit, who was studying the bulletin board, and say hi and ask her how she was doing and how Tripper liked his new home and anything else that came into his head.

But then he got yanked the other way. He couldn't do it with Shawn and Twig there. A part of him liked knowing what he knew and not letting his friends in on it: let them go crazy trying to figure it out. He knew her name, how to spell it and how to say it, and it sure wasn't anything like Pizza True Jello. He knew her father and

65

stepmother and her brothers and he had even been inside of her house. He knew about the school in Israel.

But if he let his friends know that, they'd be at him with a ton of questions, giving him a hard time. For at least a little while it was like his own secret, something they didn't have. Billy kind of enjoyed that, even if it was selfish.

Something else stopped him. His mom and dad kept saying to him and his sister, "You are known by the company you keep," which was certainly true at Jericho High School. And if kids got the idea that Pazit was really just too weird and freakish and that Billy was the only friend she had, it would not look good for him. He wasn't proud of feeling that way, but it was the truth. Billy was glad his next class was in the opposite direction and he wasn't going to have to walk past Pazit as she stood waiting at the Colonel's door.

First Day

THINGS HAD BETTER *start changing fast,* Pazit thought, *or this is not going to work.*

They didn't even *try* to pronounce her name correctly, even when she coached them.

"It's *pah-ZEET,*" she said, when the teachers got to her name in the roll call and either stopped dead or tried to fake it: *PAY-zit troo-JILL-oh.* Even when she explained about the *J* and the double *L*s, they didn't get it.

Everyone stared at her, as though she were a freak.

In the rest room before lunch some girl actually had the nerve to come up to her and say in a syrupy voice, "Don't you think that sweater is awfully revealing?"

Pazit stared at her. "No, I don't. If it's any of your business," she added.

"We don't dress that way here."

The girl sauntered off with her friends, all of them in shorts. Blood rushed to Pazit's face, and she wanted to yell after them, "At least I don't wear shorts that make my knees look like cantaloupes!"

Then in the cafeteria line some cretin with about sixty extra pounds of flab had gawked at her name, printed on her notebook, and made a big thing out of calling her "Pizza True Jello," which she tried to show she was taking as a joke, not letting him see how much it irritated her. She did not attempt to explain *anything* to that blubbery moron.

And where was Billy? Last Saturday when he mowed the lawn, he said he'd be looking for her, but so far there wasn't a sign of him. She'd been hoping all morning she'd run into him, and maybe they could eat lunch together. But the cafeteria was a madhouse, and she wasn't optimistic about finding him.

Then she spotted him, already sitting at a table. Pazit stood still, holding her tray, wishing he'd turn around and notice her. But he didn't seem to know she was there. Or if he did, he pretended he didn't.

68

Then she saw the blond girl in the drill team uniform sitting across from Billy and took in the way the girl was smiling at him, and Pazit understood why Billy wasn't noticing *her*.

Numbly, she found an empty seat and set down her tray. The other kids at the table glanced at her and looked away. To see what would happen, she asked nobody in particular, "Is it always this hot here in August?"

They looked at her blankly. "Yeah," one of them said. Then they went back to talking among themselves, pointedly ignoring her.

She picked at her food, which was even worse than she expected. Finally she gave up and went to the library to wait for her fifth period appointment with the band director.

"I just moved here from Denver," Pazit explained when Mr. Dalrymple waved her into the empty band room after fourth period. "I play flute, and I'd like to be in the band." She didn't tell him that being in a marching band had been the one thing she really enjoyed in middle school, and it was the one thing she hoped might make life bearable at Jericho High School.

"You missed band camp," said Mr. Dalrymple, a short, bald man in a greenish business suit and white sneakers. "You'd have a lot of catching up to do."

"I can do it," Pazit assured him. "I'm sure I can."

"It's not as easy as you think. For our size we're among the top marching bands in the entire state. There are many bigger bands, but none better. We know the meaning of hard work and discipline. And you're only in ninth grade! Do you have any experience in a marching band?" he asked, shuffling through her papers.

"In middle school in Denver. A lot of people said our band was better than most high-school bands. I've been studying flute since I was six, and I can memorize music really fast."

"You have your flute with you? Let me hear you play this." He propped a sheet of music on a stand and stepped back to listen, eyes half-closed. She played it well, almost perfectly.

"All right," Mr. Dalrymple said finally, handing her a red-and-white folder. "Take this music home and learn it. We don't use lyres. You're expected to have it memorized. We practice out on the field every morning at zero period and in here fourth period. Flutes are over there." He pointed to a row of empty chairs. "I'll assign your marching position tomorrow. Usually you'd have to serve as alternate for a while, but as it happens I need somebody to replace a flute who dropped out during band camp. Think you can handle it?"

"Oh, yes!"

"Then be on the field tomorrow morning, six forty-five sharp. Sit up on the bleachers and watch until I tell you different."

At least that, she told herself grimly on her way to algebra. *At least that's something.*

Fashion Statements

AFTER THE LAST bell Billy met Tanya at her locker and walked her out to the parking lot. Her mother was supposed to pick her up and drive her home, but there was no sign of Mrs. Evans's white Lincoln Continental. While they waited, Tanya talked about her classes and her friends and what the drill team instructor said, and as she chattered on Billy saw Pazit one more time, leaving through the side door: baggy black pants, holey sweater, shawl, sandals. Other girls strode past in trim shorts, suntanned bare legs gleaming, tossing their long blond hair, pretending to ignore her but *looking.* Billy watched to see if somebody had come to pick her up, but there was no sign of the VW or the station wagon. And no bicycle. It looked like she was going to *walk* home. By herself.

Tanya spotted her, too. "That girl wears a toe ring," she reported in a disgusted tone. "I saw her in the rest room. She's very strange."

"Toe ring? What are you talking about?"

"A brass ring, or maybe it's copper. On her big toe. Like something a belly dancer would wear. She wears sandals, so you can't miss it." Tanya made a face, meaning *gross.*

Tanya never wore odd clothes or strange jewelry. She and her friends dressed in designer jeans that fit perfectly or, in hot weather, tailored shorts—maximum four inches above the knee according to school rules, and they made the girls kneel and be measured if there was any doubt— ironed shirts, and clean white Reeboks. She wore a flowered dress with a lace collar and light blue shoes to church and certain school functions. On special occasions she could knock you dead in some fashion model outfit with teetery high heels that were definitely not for school. And sometimes she turned up in her Demonettes uniform. Cute, pretty, sometimes beautiful, never unusual.

"Sounds like it'd be uncomfortable," Billy said, hoping Tanya would say more about the toe ring.

"You probably get used to it, if that's how you're brought up," Tanya said. "At least it's not

73

a nose ring. She's definitely a foreigner. I heard she's from Israel. A Jew, you know? I wouldn't be surprised if she doesn't even speak English."

Billy opened his mouth to say, "Of course she speaks English," but then he'd have to explain how he knew that, and that would lead to more questions, more explanations. So he shut his mouth again. He was going to have to figure a way to handle this.

Tanya hung on his arm, so close he was breathing in her sweet perfume. They waited while a couple of school buses wheezed past, headed for the loading zone behind the school to pick up the bus kids. Not many of the students rode the bus, except black kids who lived clear on the other side of town and didn't have their own cars.

First thing after you turned sixteen in Jericho, you got a car. Before that you rode a bicycle, or somebody picked you up—not your mother, you hoped, although Tanya's mom always did. The best deal was to have a friend with a car who would drive you around in return for gas money. One reason Billy was friends with Twig Terwilliger was that Twig owned a maroon 1980 Oldsmobile, and he'd drive you almost anywhere for a buck. Billy would turn sixteen on November twelfth, which meant he had less than two months until he could get his license. The problem was not the license; it was the car and the insurance. He had been saving for two years, putting away part of whatever he earned mowing lawns, and he still had a long way to go.

Mrs. Evans's Lincoln glided into the pick-up lane. Tanya reached up to plant a kiss on Billy's cheek and ran to get in. Next June, when Tanya turned sixteen, Tanya would have her own car. Her parents had promised her a new Honda. Mrs. Evans waved and smiled at him through the window she kept closed to prevent the A.C. from leaking out, and they drove away.

Billy walked slowly to the bike rack, rubbing his cheek in case there was lipstick on it, still thinking about what Tanya had told him about the toe ring. For a little bit he thought about catching up with Pazit and walking her the rest of the way home, so she wouldn't have to be alone.

But then Billy checked his watch, the one his parents had given him last Christmas, with a stop-watch and alarm. It even had an altimeter and a compass, in case he was ever lost in the wilderness. Altitude of Jericho: 432'; time: 3:24 P.M.; date: TUE 8/24. Better get on home, he decided. Billy swung his leg over the crossbar and leaned into the pedals, heading uptown toward Pennsylvania.

No Jews in Jericho

DAY TWO DID not go any better than Day One. It was beginning to dawn on Pazit that it might have been a mistake to come to Jericho, a mistake to think she could actually *live* in a town like this, a mistake to have promised she'd stay for a whole school year. She'd made the promise when she was desperate to get away from Denver. How was she to know it would be like this?

Jericho High School was ludicrous. The students were ludicrous. The teachers were ludicrous. She could not believe the things they said to her, the absurd questions they asked.

Coming out of biology, one of the girls said,

"Oh, so you're Mexican," and Pazit replied, "No, I'm not Mexican, I'm an American like you. I was born in Denver, Colorado, and I lived there for thirteen years."

As though Pazit hadn't even opened her mouth, another girl said, "We heard you're Jewish," and Pazit said, "I *am* Jewish. What's that got to do with anything?"

"There aren't any Jews in this school," said the girl, staring at her with flat, expressionless eyes. Without another word they turned away and left her standing alone.

This morning at six forty-five, thick-headed and grumpy from getting up so early, she had reported to the marching field. But she was impressed by what she saw and heard. Billy was right—this band was *good*. She felt a little flutter of excitement that she would be part of it. She had no trouble spotting Billy and his bass drum out on the field. The blubbery one was there, too, a pair of cymbals in his pudgy hands. If she had no trouble spotting *Billy*, surely he had no trouble spotting *her*.

Band members flocked noisily into the band room after lunch. Lunch had been another disaster—horrible food eaten in isolation, as though she had a disease. Pazit, sitting among the flutes, looked over at Billy in percussion and willed him to look her way, but he did not. What was going on here? Pazit wondered. He was still ignoring her, and his girlfriend was nowhere in sight.

Mr. Dalrymple began whipping down the list of ninety-six last names without a pause until he got to the *T*s. Then there was a snag and out came *"troo-JILL-o?"* even though she had explained it all to him yesterday. Finally she said "Here," and he raced on through Tucker and Turner and Tyler.

"Take out your first number," the director instructed. " 'Onward, Christian Soldiers.' Horns first."

When it was the flutes' turn, Pazit read her part easily. Finally they put all the sections together, standing up and marching in place. Mr. Dalrymple bawled them out for general sloppiness, and they moved on to the next piece of music, "Amazing Grace."

Pazit turned to the flutist on her left. "You always play so many hymns?" she asked.

The girl looked at Pazit as though she had just asked why so many people were speaking English. "Mr. Dalrymple is a Christian. He believes in playing Christian music."

The last straw, Pazit thought grimly, *the absolute last straw.* But she put the flute to her lips and played her line.

On the way home she made up her mind to

tell them nothing. For the first couple of weeks after she'd arrived, when she was at home with the little guys and Tripper, everything had been fine. Her father had joked about Jericho—"the buckle on the Bible Belt," he'd called it—but she'd figured she could deal with it, keep her part of the bargain, and if she didn't like it she could leave as soon as school ended next spring. But after yesterday and now today, it was obvious there was no way she could last an entire nine months.

"How was school?" Ellen would inquire, and later her father would ask, "How did it go?"

"OK," she would say. Period.

She sped through the hall past the living room, past the dining room, and had almost made it to the stairs leading up to her own room when her stepmother intercepted her.

"Zeetie? That you?"

"Yes, it's me."

Ellen came out of her studio off the kitchen, a smudge of clay on her cheek, her face crinkled in a big smile. "So how was school?" Ellen asked cheerfully.

"OK," Pazit said.

"Good." Ellen blocked her path. "Let me wash my hands and we'll have some iced tea and you can tell me about it."

Trapped.

Ellen poured sun tea into slightly lopsided mugs, ones she'd made that hadn't turned out quite right, and perched a slice of lemon on each rim. Pazit concentrated on stirring sugar into hers. Before Ellen could ask a question, Brian and Matt came running in from playing in the backyard. Their school got out earlier than Pazit's, and already they were sweaty and dirty. They clambered onto chairs at the kitchen table and slurped juice, watching Pazit over the rims of their plastic cups with big, solemn eyes.

Pazit stared back at the boys, angry at them for no reason. She was angry at Ellen, too, also for no reason except that she was here. In fact, Pazit was angry at the whole situation. Why had her father moved out here, anyway? Why hadn't they just stayed in Colorado? The Springs was a much better place to live. If he didn't have these two kids, there might have been enough money to keep her in school in Israel for another year. If he had stayed married to her mother, everything would have been different. Ruth would have refused to move to Jericho. She would have told Gus, "I won't live in a town where there are no Jews," and that would have settled it, job or no job.

Ellen hadn't refused. For one thing, Ellen wasn't Jewish. And Gus wasn't Jewish. So the little guys weren't Jewish, and nobody had to worry about *them*. Possibly they didn't even notice that there weren't any Jews. Maybe that's why Pazit was furious with all of them. What she wasn't ready to admit to herself was that she was also furious at herself: if she had studied harder she would have gotten her scholarship renewed and she'd still be in Israel.

"My classes are extremely boring," Pazit told Ellen, sucking on the lemon slice. "I've had all this stuff before, in Israel, but they're making me take it over."

"Well then, this time you should ace it all," Ellen said, mopping up the juice Brian had spilled.

"Who cares about acing anything!" She hadn't intended to sound so mad, but it was a ridiculous argument. Tears crowded up as though they had been waiting all day.

The little guys looked at her, surprised, then at their mother, who pursed her lips. They begged for peanut-butter crackers, and when Ellen went to get them, Pazit escaped up the stairs to her room and locked the door.

Her orange shawl with glittering gold threads was draped over hooks she'd screwed into the frame above the door, so that the shawl hung down like a curtain. The effect was like entering a tent. She shrugged out of her green skirt and sleeveless blouse and let them fall on the floor. She pulled on a pair of ragged cutoffs, an unironed top, and her worn-out Converse high-tops and went back down to the kitchen.

Ellen wasn't around; back in her studio throwing pots, no doubt. Pazit was supposed to play with the little guys from after school until dinner. She was also supposed to do the boys' laundry twice a week as well as her own and to load and unload the dishwasher every day. Those were her chores.

In Israel she had gotten occasional reprimands: "shirks her chores." Everybody had jobs, some awful, some not so bad. Catching chickens for the *Shabbat* dinner—that was the one Pazit always shirked. She couldn't stand the struggle of the panicky chicken in her arms, knowing she was carrying it to its doom. Looking after a pair of little brothers was, by comparison, not bad.

After the coolness of the air-conditioned house, the backyard was stifling. Tripper heard her coming and flung himself against the gate of his new dog run, barking joyously.

Pazit went to pick up his dish and water bucket, the little guys shoving ahead of her into the pen. Tripper, sensing opportunity, came blasting through the gate the instant it opened and raced down the driveway, his ears flattened, headed for the street and freedom and danger.

"Tripper, no!" Pazit hollered. She paused long

enough to yell, "Brian, Matt, you stay there! I'll be right back!" then took off after him.

Tripper raced down Fourth Street, stopping every once in a while to look back and make sure she was still following him. As soon as she got close, the dog leaped away again. She could see him almost laughing at her, having so much fun.

Her high-tops slapping on the hot pavement, Pazit trotted steadily after him as he headed downtown toward the square, as though he knew exactly where he was going. Suddenly he veered, dashing out into the busy street. There was a sickening screech of brakes. "Oh *no!*" she cried, covering her eyes.

When she dared to look, the car was stopped, cutting off the dog's escape route, but it hadn't hit him. Pazit was trembling. Two girls Pazit vaguely recognized from school stared out at her, open-mouthed. The driver wound down the car window and called out, "Is your dog OK? I didn't hit him, did I?"

"No, he's fine," Pazit said. The dog's tongue was lolling, and he yawned deeply. "Thank you," she added. "Tripper, come here," she coaxed in a shaky voice, remembering from the book her father had bought that you had to speak nicely if you wanted a dog to come. He looked at her with his dimwitted doggy smile, waiting for her to make a dive for his collar so he could dodge away again.

The car drove off. Pazit managed to seize Tripper and drag him out of the street, her fingers hooked in his collar. She was still shaking.

When her father came home, she braced herself for another round of questions. "How did it go, *mi hijita?*" he asked, turning on the television to watch the five-thirty news. Brian curled up next to him on the lumpy couch in the TV room. Ellen came in with a beer for Gus and a glass of wine for herself and settled on the floor, leaning back against his legs. Matt crawled onto her lap.

The TV voice was already saying, "Good evening, this is NBC News. I'm Tom Brokaw."

It was a ritual. Pazit had figured out this was something they had been doing day after day, since long before she got here. She poured herself a glass of juice and squeezed in next to her father on the couch. She thought the news was pretty boring, but she did like sitting close to him.

"Tripper runned away," Brian said, patting his father's cheek to get his attention.

"But Zeetie catched him," Matt added.

"Unfortunately," Ellen said, sipping her wine. Pazit knew that Ellen was actually getting fond of the dog, but she still didn't like to admit it.

"Gotta keep that gate closed, fellas," Gus said,

his mind already on a report from the White House.

During the commercial break he asked again, "So how was school, *mi hijita?*"

"It was OK," she lied.

Cross Marching

"BAND!" MR. DALRYMPLE barked over his field mike.

"Sir!" snapped ninety-six members of the Jericho High School Marching Band.

Seven o'clock in the morning, and already sweat was dripping off Billy's nose. Billy shifted his bass drum, easing the back sling that bit into his shoulders, and waited for the next order.

BOOM-boom-boom-boom, Billy kept the beat going steady as a clock, his eye on Mr. Dalrymple, thinking about where his own feet were supposed to be from one beat to the next. Everybody was concentrating on taking eight steps from yardline to yardline, each step exactly twenty-two-and-a-half inches.

They were still practicing the intricate pattern of steps that would propel them down the football field at halftime at the Friday night games. Only two more weeks until the opening game, and by *dang* they'd better have it down perfect! No screw-ups, not even minor ones, or the Colonel would be on their case, yelling at them something terrible: Where were their brains? Where was their school spirit? How could they let everybody down by performing like a bunch of fools—like they were from some third-rate school that didn't have a reputation like Jericho's to live up to?

Billy could not resist glancing over at Pazit. She must have convinced the Colonel she could do it, because here she was. She carried her flute in position but wasn't playing because they weren't supposed to play yet. He could see that she was struggling to keep up with their moves. The other flutes should have been helping her, coaching her along, but it didn't look like they were.

The routine started out with lines of marchers weaving in and out while they played an upbeat version of "Amazing Grace." That was a crowd-pleaser, Mr. Dalrymple told them; the band had done it a few years back and the audience loved it.

He had had so many requests for it that he had decided this year to build the music and the routine around a Christian theme. Last year, it was all cowboys and western stuff. The year before that it was patriotic, forming a flag that seemed actually to wave as they marched down the field. Theme was important in winning competitions, Mr. Dalrymple reminded them.

As usual the Colonel had come up with something entirely original this season. They'd do their weaving, form a pattern and then dissolve it, move into something else and dissolve, from "Amazing Grace" right through "Precious Lord, Take My Hand," to parts of "Onward, Christian Soldiers" in quickstep and then the finale, "A Mighty Fortress Is Our God," when they'd change to a stately kick step and form a giant cross that would move majestically across the field and end up right in front of the stands. This kind of dramatic routine had become the trademark of the Jericho High School Marching Band, the kind of thing that had taken them to state finals nine years in a row.

It wasn't easy; it took diligent effort, and Mr. Dalrymple was always on them, making them work even harder: "Perfection! Nothing short of perfection!" Next to the football coach, the band director was probably the most important person in the whole school, Billy thought, and maybe, during the football season, in the entire town. Even if the Jericho football team didn't manage to win every single game or, in bad years, even half of their games, the marching band could always be counted on to bring home a trophy. The trophy case in the main hall of the school displayed their triumphs.

Twenty-five years ago Billy's dad, Richard Harper, had been a star running back for the Jericho Demons, and he probably figured his sons would follow in his footsteps. Billy's brother, Richie Junior, had done it; he'd even gotten a football scholarship to Tech. But no matter how many times Richard Harper had taken Billy out to toss around a football, it never seemed to go right. Billy always ended up in tears, or close to it—his dad would have had a fit if he had caught him actually crying. Same thing with baseball. His dad signed him up for Little League, but Billy spent most of the time waiting for a turn at bat that seldom came.

"The boy just doesn't have any *ball* sense," Richard Senior complained to Billy's mom, his disappointment written plain as newspaper headlines across his face.

And Virginia Harper, who played piano for the Wednesday night Prayer and Praise service and also sang in the church choir, had pretty much given up on Billy's musical ability, too, when the clarinet teacher called her in and said it wasn't that Billy didn't try, but his embouchure was terrible: he just couldn't seem to blow right.

It was Billy's idea to take up the bass drum when his friend Shawn Stovall did, a way to get into the band and maybe the only way he could prove to his parents that he was just as loyal to Jericho High School as they were, as Richie was. Just as loyal as his sister, Brenda, who was a senior and a lieutenant of the Demonettes. People thought it didn't take any musical talent to play a bass drum, but it did: you had to have a good sense of tempo and be able keep a steady beat, not speed up or slow down, so the marchers would always know *exactly* when their feet were supposed to hit the ground. And you definitely had to pay attention. That, Billy could do.

"The discipline is what I want for you," Billy's dad had said often. He'd repeated it again last night when they were finishing supper, about to leave for Jericho Bible Temple. "Kids nowadays don't get enough discipline. Not like when I was a youngster, I can tell you."

BOOM-boom-boom-boom, Billy pounded the drum, keeping the strict four/four time, his feet on automatic pilot as he maneuvered through the steps. He'd practiced these moves so often he could do them in his sleep. He wished he could wipe the sweat off his face.

"People, you're thinking too much!" Mr. Dalrymple bellowed when they had screwed up again, the trumpets somehow heading off in the wrong direction. "By this time you shouldn't have to think at all! The time for thinking is past! It should be habit by now! If you're making mistakes it's because you're still *thinking!* All right, take your position at the end of the last phrase and get ready to move into the cross."

That was when Billy noticed that Pazit had quit marching and was standing on the sidelines. She was wearing another goofy outfit—not the floppy pants this time, but a droopy skirt over white leggings that looked like long underwear. She stood quietly, like she was waiting for them to stop whatever foolishness they were up to.

Mr. Dalrymple noticed her, too. "Flute?" he called out. He never bothered to learn anybody's name. You could be in the band all four years of your high-school career, and on the day you graduated, played "Pomp and Circumstance," and then went up on the stage to get your diploma, the Colonel still probably wouldn't know your name. Ninety-six was a lot of names to remember, but *still.* On the other hand, Billy thought, maybe she'd rather be called "Flute" than some awful mispronunciation of her name.

The rest of them kept on marching, and Billy

kept on pounding his bass drum, weaving in and out. Any minute now Mr. Dalrymple would tell them they had to play, too, and then they'd have to remember it all, their notes as well as their steps.

Billy's line of marchers made a sharp left-face, headed for the cross. He was now in front of Shawn, the second bass drummer. Shawn's lips moved as he counted the beat. Billy slid his eyes toward Pazit, and Shawn followed his glance and shrugged.

Then they were into the cross, doing the difficult kick step that drove Mr. Dalrymple wild because they had such a hard time kicking at the same precise angle. Mr. Dalrymple blew his whistle, two shorts and a long, and everybody took two more in-place steps and halted. "Five-minute break," he announced. "Then we do it with music."

Just because you had a five-minute break didn't mean you could go anywhere. The band members sagged onto the ground, baked dry and hard from the relentless sun and lack of rain. Twig, his T-shirt soaked through, stretched out flat, like a big whale, with a huge brass cymbal on each side. Shawn and Billy sat with their elbows on their knees, gawking like everyone else as Mr. Dalrymple went over to talk to Pazit.

The director flapped his arms up and down a couple of times in that odd way he had, talking intensely, his face close to hers. She stood with her feet planted apart and her arms folded across her chest, looking him right in the eye. If anything he said bothered her, she didn't show it. *Pretty brave,* Billy thought.

"Wonder what that's all about?" Shawn murmured.

But before Billy could come up with an answer, Mr. Dalrymple blew his whistle and they scrambled to their feet.

"Band!"

"Sir!"

" 'A Mighty Fortress.' With instruments, please. And watch the position of those toes!"

The giant cross began to move, without Pazit. She stood right where she was, playing but not marching one step.

BY THE END of school that day everybody had heard the story, or some version of it: Pizza True Jello—as Twig had everyone calling her—had told Mr. Dalrymple she wouldn't march in a cross. Suzanne Higgins, who played trombone, claimed she had overheard most of their conversation.

"She said, 'Mr. Dalrymple, I don't feel comfortable marching in that cross. I'm Jewish, and I don't believe in Jesus or the cross.' Then she told him she didn't think he had any right to force her to march in a cross if she didn't want to, that there was such a thing as freedom of religion, and she would never try to make him or anyone else in the band march in a Star of David if that was against their religion. And he said yes, that was true, there was freedom of religion, and who was she to try to force her beliefs on everyone else? If that was her attitude, then she better just drop out of the band. And she answered him right back, can you believe it? She told him she wasn't going to drop out, that she had a right to play. Finally he gave in and said she didn't have to march, she could just stand on the sidelines and play, which I think is totally ridiculous, don't you?"

As the story spread, details changed. Billy heard several versions. Some claimed that Pizza True Jello had told the Colonel the whole band had to march in a Star of David, or she wouldn't do the cross. Billy didn't know what to think.

Tanya was furious. "I told you she was a Jew," Tanya said to Billy as they walked to her mother's car, and Billy didn't contradict her. "I think she ought to get out of Jericho, pack her bags, and go back to Israel or New York or wherever it is she belongs."

"Maybe she'll change," Billy said.

"Not her," Tanya replied. "Never her kind."

Billy hated it when Tanya got like this: so stubborn, so unreasonable. Talk about never changing! You couldn't convince Tanya that anything might be the least bit different than the way she made up her mind it was. It would be like arguing with Mrs. Shoemaker that Pazit wasn't a communist.

"I guess you'd know," he said.

She looked at him, surprised. "What's that supposed to mean?"

He shrugged. "Nothing. I'll see you tomorrow, OK?"

Billy twirled the combination lock on his bike and wheeled it out of the rack, glad there was only one more day of school this week. He was definitely ready for the weekend.

Keeping Kosher

"Zeetie? That you?"

"Yes, it's me."

This time she would *not* keep quiet. After her father came home from teaching his classes, after the nightly ritual of the national news and the local weather report, when they were eating dinner and her father asked his usual "How did it go today, *mi hijita?*" she would tell them exactly how it went. *Bad.*

She made it safely through the kitchen and rushed out the back door before Ellen had time to get out of her studio. She called over her shoulder, "I'm going to give Tripper a bath."

Brian and Matt loved that idea. They helped

her lug out the blue plastic tub and fill it. Pazit lured the reluctant dog into the water and held him by his collar while the little guys took turns soaping him up and squirting him with the garden hose. Tripper endured it patiently until he suddenly lunged out of the tub, splashing them all, and shook himself violently.

When Pazit went back into the house soaking wet, Ellen looked at her and frowned. "I know, I know," Pazit said before Ellen could utter a word. She ran up to her room, peeled off the muddy skirt and soggy leggings and pulled on her favorite ragged cutoffs, which she knew she should have changed into in the first place.

Next she went to work on the salad for dinner, cutting up raw vegetables into small, even pieces—the way her mother did, the way people fixed salads in Israel—not those big pieces of lettuce the size of your hand and huge chunks of mushroom and bell peppers, the way Americans made salads.

She was starving. School food was indescribably awful. Everything on the menu seemed to have ham or bacon in it or cheese piled on the chicken or beef. She'd settled on double-cheese pizza three days in a row. That was probably all she'd ever get to eat there.

Everything else stayed the same, too. Each day she recognized a few more people in her classes, a few more in the band. But they ignored her, behaving as though she didn't exist. Especially Billy, and until today she couldn't figure it out. By turns it made her feel angry, hurt, and confused.

She'd seen him several times—on the field, in the band room, in the cafeteria. At first she'd hoped he'd invite her to come and join him and his girlfriend, that silly Tanya who was in her theater class, and the freckled kid who played the other bass drum and the blimpy one and his girlfriend, a friend of Tanya's.

But he didn't, and Pazit knew now that he wouldn't do anything like that with all his friends around. Not after what happened this morning out on the field when she explained to Mr. Dalrymple why she couldn't march in the cross. So she ate by herself again, telling herself it wasn't that big a deal. But if it wasn't, why did her stomach hurt so much?

The television clicked off as soon as the weather report ended and sports came on. Ellen decided it was too hot to eat outside on the patio, so Pazit helped Brian and Matt set the kitchen table. Brian put the knives where the forks were supposed to be and vice versa, and Pazit switched them. Matt began folding paper napkins in triangles, concentrating as though he were making origami. Gus wandered into the kitchen murmuring, "Good smells!" and popped another beer and refilled El-len's wine glass. Pazit got her salad out of the re-frigerator and doused it with dressing. Ellen began dishing up lasagna. Pazit poured milk for the little guys and orange juice for herself. They sat down at their usual places.

Pazit probed the lasagna and saw that her step-mother had forgotten again that the combination of meat and cheese wasn't kosher. She decided not to say anything. Salad would be enough.

"So how did it go today, *mi hijita?*" her father asked, right on schedule. "Got any good stories for us?"

"As a matter of fact," she said, "I do."

"Let's hear it," Ellen said.

She had been preparing for this moment all day. "Well, as you know, I went to band practice this morning at zero hour—that's what they call the period before regular classes start. They were rehearsing their marching formation for the half-time program. It's a very *interesting* formation. Very interesting *indeed.*" Pazit speared an olive slice, pausing to build up the dramatic tension and sa-voring the moment.

Gus glanced up and adjusted his glasses. "Oh? How so?"

"You've got us on pins and needles," Ellen said, cutting up Brian's noodles.

"The band is playing all Christian hymns," Pazit continued, "and they're marching in a giant cross."

Her father blinked. "A cross?"

"You know, like a Jesus cross? We're playing 'Amazing Grace,' plus a couple of other hymns, like 'Precious Lord, Take My Hand.' And then as we go into 'Onward, Christian Soldiers,' we form this huge cross"—demonstrating with her hands how huge it was—"and march across the field for the grand finale."

Ellen laid down her fork. "I can't believe this. A *cross*? Who is this guy, Zeetie?"

She shrugged. "His name is Mr. Dalrymple. I don't know much about him. He's pretty strict, that's all I know. The kids call him the Colonel."

Then she repeated the conversation they'd had that morning on the edge of the field, which she thought she'd handled very well. "I told him I didn't want to march in a cross because I'm Jewish, and he said it's too late now to change anything, because he worked this whole routine out last spring and they've been practicing for weeks, since way before school started. The first game is two weeks from tomorrow, and then in October they have the regional competitions, which the Jericho band always wins. He told me I can stand on the sidelines or sit in the stands if I don't want to march, but he's not changing the routine."

"Baloney," said her father. "I'm going to go talk to him."

"Oh please, Dad, no!" Pazit hadn't expected her story to take this turn. She wanted her father's sympathy. She wanted him to say what a brave thing she had done, sticking up for her rights. But she hadn't expected him to actually *do* something. Pazit didn't think of her father as a man of action—mostly he liked to lecture and discuss endlessly, and mostly she tuned him out. But she sensed that this time it might be different. "I think you should stay out of it, Dad," she said, trying to sound calm and reasonable. "I really don't think you should get involved."

"But what your Mr. Dalrymple is doing is unconstitutional. He's probably some kind of religious nut. He shouldn't be allowed to get away with this."

"I think she's right, Gus," Ellen said. "You don't want to go charging in there. Everybody's going to know who's stirring up trouble. It could make life pretty unpleasant for Zeetie."

Pazit looked at her stepmother gratefully. This was not the time to tell her she didn't like being called Zeetie.

"So what are you going to do?" Pazit asked uneasily.

"Well, if you don't want me to go see him, then there might be another way—through legal channels. That way there's no personal confrontation. The thing is, what he's doing is in direct conflict with the First Amendment to the United States Constitution that guarantees freedom of religion through the separation of church and state. It's not freedom of religion when the band director in a public high school, supported by taxpayers money, forces students to play Christian hymns and participate in Christian symbols. If you have to march in a cross in order to be in the band, then that's wrong. Your civil liberties are being violated, sweetheart. And so are the civil liberties of anyone else in the band who has different views."

"But he's not forcing me to do anything," Pazit protested. She hated it when her father lectured like this, and there was nothing she could say back. "And I'm the only one with different views. Everybody else is a Christian."

"Are you serious?" Ellen asked. *"Everybody?"*

"That's what some girls told me. They said there aren't any Jews in Jericho High School."

"I find that hard to believe. But how about Muslims? Or Hindus? Or just plain old atheists, people who don't believe in any religion at all?"

"I don't *know!*" Pazit cried. "All I know is that nobody else in the band seems to care except me."

Gus reached across the table and squeezed Pazit's hand in both of his. "Listen, I know you don't want to start a big ruckus, and I don't blame you. I'm just going to find out if there's a local ACLU chapter in Jericho and make a few discreet inquiries. It's possible they already know about this band director."

"What's that?" she asked. "ACLU?"

"American Civil Liberties Union. It's a group that focuses on the Bill of Rights. They're often called in when there are problems like this. I promise I won't do anything further without your permission, how's that?"

"OK, I guess," she said with a sigh.

They went back to their meal. Gus reached for the salad. Matt was meticulously picking microscopic bits of onion out of the tomato sauce on the lasagna. He had already removed every trace of olive from the spoonful of salad on his plate.

"Come on, Matt," Ellen said. "Just eat it, OK?" Then her attention shifted. "Aren't you going to have some lasagna, Zeetie?"

"No thanks." She decided to come right out and say why. "It's got meat and cheese in it. I don't eat meat and dairy at the same meal."

"Oh, I'm *sorry!* Where was my head?" Ellen

smacked her forehead. "Can I get you something else?"

"It's OK." That was the trouble with saying something to Ellen. She always took it so personally, so hard, when she failed at being a Good Stepmother, that you felt like apologizing to her. "And also," she said, "would you mind not calling me Zeetie? It's OK if the little guys do, but my name is *Pazit*."

IN HER ROOM after dinner while the dishwasher churned in the kitchen and Gus had gone outside with the little guys to water Ellen's plants, Pazit practiced her flute. It was what she often did when she was upset about something. When she and her mother had their horrendous fights, both of them yelling until they were hoarse, Pazit always retreated into her music.

She spread the band's hymns across her bed and played through her part in each of them. The music was easy enough; she already had most of it memorized, and it was really kind of fun to play. She didn't know the words, since she wasn't familiar with the hymns the way everybody else seemed to be, but she really didn't mind playing the notes. It was the cross that bothered her. The music could be anything at all, but the cross was the cross.

She wished she hadn't said anything to her father and Ellen. *Maybe,* she tried to convince herself, *nothing will come of this.* All she could do was hope they'd get busy and distracted and forget about it.

She was working on "Amazing Grace" when the phone rang. She didn't bother to answer it, because it was never for her, but then she heard Ellen call from the bottom of the stairs. "Pazit! Phone!"

She ran to Gus's study across the hall and picked up the extension.

"Hey," said a male voice. "This is Billy."

"Yes?" she said coolly.

"Well, I was just calling to say hi, what's up, see how you're doing and all." His voice squeaked, as though he was nervous.

"I'm fine," she said.

"Uh, well, good. So, how's Tripper? Does he like his house?"

"He likes it fine." She was about to tell him how Tripper had managed to escape the day before, but then she thought about how Billy had ignored her at school when his friends were around, and her anger surged up and stopped her cold.

"Did you call for some reason?" she asked finally.

But before he could answer, if he even had an answer, the call-waiting signal beeped. "I have to go," she said. "There's another call coming in." Abruptly she cut him off and answered the next call. It was for her father.

Pazit went outside and hollered for him. He picked up in the kitchen, and before she hung up the phone in his study, she caught his first few words: "Jack, who's the contact here for the ACLU, do you know? I think we've got a situation. . . ."

Gently she placed the receiver back in the cradle. Other people were going to know about this now. It wasn't just the band, or just her family. With a growing heaviness in the pit of her stomach, Pazit went back to her room and picked up her flute. No more "Amazing Grace," though. She put away the hymns and searched for some Vivaldi.

Fishing

NO MATTER WHAT he tried to do, he ended up putting his foot in his mouth.

Tanya was totally wrapped up in making the Demonette senior squad. Friday night he'd gone over to her house with Twig and Ashleigh to watch videos, and all the girls could talk about was their Demonette routines. Billy was sick of hearing about it. Later, as they sat in the dark watching some movie he couldn't even remember afterward and he started kissing her, Tanya acted like nothing at all was happening, like she had forgotten he was even there. He would have left right then, if he had his own car. But of course he had to wait for Twig, who was in no hurry to go anywhere.

Then Tanya showed up at Billy's house on Saturday morning, dropped off by her mother, before they had even finished breakfast, to practice with Brenda. Tanya was all smiles, like she knew he was mad about the night before and was trying to make it up to him. His mother, who thought Tanya was practically perfect because her father was a lawyer and a leader of the county Prayer in the Schools Committee, insisted that she sit down and have some pancakes with them. But Billy got the sudden feeling that the smiles and sweet looks she was giving him had more to do with the fact that he was Brenda Harper's brother—Lieutenant Brenda would have something to say about whether Tanya Evans made the senior Demonettes—than it did with him.

Saturday was Chore Day, another effect of his mother going to work. After breakfast Billy stripped all the beds, dumped a load of sheets and towels in the washer, and made up the beds again. Brenda was supposed to vacuum and dust, but she was out in the backyard doing precision kicks with Tanya. He and Brenda took turns cleaning the bathroom they shared, each one blaming the other one for leaving it a mess. This was Billy's week, and he swished through it as fast as he could.

Later in the morning, to get away from the leaping, yelling Demonettes in the backyard, he rode his bike down to the Shoemakers'. When he'd finished their yard, he'd gone next door, and there was Mrs. Trujillo with the mower repaired and an almost-new edger and hedge clippers she'd bought at a garage sale. No sign of Pazit, but he hadn't really expected her to come out. Not after that phone call Thursday night.

He should have known the phone call was a bad idea, since A) he had pretty much ignored her in school for three days, and B) she had made such a stink about the band's marching program and got everybody upset. He thought maybe she'd be glad to have somebody call her up and let her know that even if he didn't agree with her, he still thought she was fine. More than fine. He felt kind of stupid afterward, sorry he had bothered. But he couldn't really blame her for blowing him off.

Then at band practice yesterday morning he'd watched her standing on the sidelines with her flute. He'd looked right at her, but she didn't give any sign that she even noticed him. He decided he wouldn't try to call her again.

When Billy finished the yard work and rang the bell, Mrs. Trujillo came to the door herself. She didn't say anything about Pazit, and Billy didn't ask. Once more she paid him more than she owed him.

"Thank you, ma'am," he said.

"Next week?" she asked.

"Yes, ma'am."

SUNDAY MORNING, in the Senior High Bible Study Class, they studied Matthew 28:16: Go, then, to all peoples everywhere and make them my disciples. Then Brother Kent Secrist showed a video about how it was everybody's job to spread the word of Jesus, the *knowledge* of Jesus. In the video a bunch of people were tossing fish into a lake, while a voice-over explained that bringing people to Jesus was a lot like stocking a lake with walleyed pike.

"Throw in just a few fish," the narrator had assured them, "and the pike will start multiplying on their own." In the same way, he said, you need only a few Christians in any group to start moving people toward the Lord. In fact, all you really need in a group is *one person* who truly loves Jesus, and that's enough to start turning that whole group toward the Lord.

"OK," said Brother Kent when the light switch had been flipped back on, "I want each of you to think of a group you belong to where you can start bringing folks to Jesus. Because that's what we're all about here at Bible Temple, remember that."

Billy tried to think of a likely group. Trouble was, in any group he belonged to, everybody was already a Christian. Everybody he knew went to church every Sunday, and Wednesday nights, too.

Maybe not everybody! Billy's mind had jumped to Pazit. He sucked in his breath, making such an odd sound that Brother Kent looked straight at him. "Billy? Can you think of a group where you might start bringing folks to the Lord?"

Billy shook his head, hating to be called on. But when Brother Kent was talking about all the kinds of people who needed to be brought to Jesus, like the Chinese and the Hindus in India and the African tribes who didn't have any religion at all, Billy raised his hand. "What about Jewish people?" he asked.

"Well, *sure,* we want to bring Jews to the Lord!" Brother Kent exclaimed. "Don't forget, Jesus is their Messiah. He's already their Lord and Savior, but they just don't know it yet!"

Billy slumped down in his chair, hoping Brother Kent wouldn't ask him anything else. Billy had all kinds of questions he didn't know how to ask, like how was he to go about doing such a thing? Or should he even try?

Among the questions was what Tanya, who was practically Miss Mission Hill Christian Teen herself, would say if she found out Billy was fishing for Pazit's soul.

Later in church, when they were to pray for

their own particular needs, Billy decided to take his questions to the Lord, as he had been taught all his life. "Just tell it to Jesus," his mom always said. "He'll help you. Trust Him."

Help me, Jesus, he prayed. *It's me, Billy Harper, and I don't know what to do.*

Ulterior Motives

ELLEN SCOOPED UP salsa with a corn chip. "Now that Billy Harper," Ellen said, "is a very cute boy. Not exactly a *hunk,* maybe, but awfully cute. And so nice and polite! It's like a dream, Gus! First he builds the doghouse. Then he shows up again just as the mower quits and gets it started, finishes mowing front *and* back, and yesterday he's back to do the edging and clipping. For five bucks an hour."

"Sounds like a great bargain," said Gus, painting a row of drumsticks on the grill with orangy sauce.

"I suspect ulterior motives," Ellen said.

"Such as?" Gus rearranged the chicken and painted the other side.

"Don't be dense. He's got eyes for our daughter, of course."

Yeeeeesh! Pazit glared at Ellen, willing her to shut up. Her father grinned and waggled his eyebrows. "Smart kid, that Billy. And are you likewise interested in him?"

"No," she said, hoping that would end it. She should have known better.

"But why not?" Ellen asked. "This really *sweet* boy shows up on your doorstep and you brush him off like an annoying insect. You were nicer to your stupid dog when he first came to the door."

"I'm not brushing him off," Pazit insisted impatiently. "You asked me if I was interested, and I said no, because I'm not, that's all." She wished she didn't have to keep explaining herself to Ellen. Ellen never seemed to get particularly upset—she didn't have Ruth's short fuse and never lost her temper—but she kept *poking* at things. "I hardly know him. He's in the band," Pazit added sullenly. "That's about all I know about him."

"Uh-oh," Ellen said, glancing at Gus. "I forgot about that. Billy being in the band."

Pazit caught the look that passed between them. "What?" she asked, suddenly tense. "What's going on?"

"Well," her father began, "it looks as though things are starting to move. I talked to a friend of mine, Professor Salisbury, on Thursday, and he put me in touch with the head of the local ACLU chapter, Mrs. Lovett. And I told her about your problem with the band marching in a cross."

"It's not *my* problem, Dad," Pazit said, an edge of anger creeping into her voice. "I just told Mr. Dalrymple I wasn't going to do it, and he agreed that I could stand on the sidelines, or else sit in the stands, and play my flute."

"But is that what you want to do, Pazit? Stand on the sidelines while everybody else is out on the field marching?"

"Well, no, of course not. Sure, I'd rather march. But not in a cross. And since everybody else is doing the cross, I guess that leaves me out. Majority rule or something." Her stomach was doing peculiar, jumpy things, the way it did when she was upset.

"That's exactly why I called the ACLU, Pazit. You shouldn't be left out because of what you believe. This is a violation of your First Amendment rights."

"So what does Billy have to say about this?" Ellen asked. Brian came and climbed on Ellen's lap.

Billy again! Billy who was a great friend when he was here at her house but didn't know her from

115

dirt when they were at school. "I haven't talked to him about it. I haven't talked to anybody about it, except Mr. Dalrymple. But you can figure that Billy isn't that much different from everybody else in the band."

"He just seems like such a neat kid!" Ellen insisted, handing Brian a chip.

"I wish you would stop saying that! So he's neat, so what difference does that make?" Pazit demanded, close to tears. Billy wasn't as neat as Ellen thought, or he wouldn't be ignoring her at school, but Pazit didn't feel like telling them about that. This whole business was making her sick. "Everybody in the band wants the cross. Everybody in the whole school probably wants the cross. Including Billy. Anyway, he already has a girlfriend. You should see Tanya. Blond hair and big blue eyes and just so *ooh ooh ooh*," Pazit said and jumped up and minced across the brick patio, swinging her hips, to demonstrate Tanya's *ooh*-ness. Focusing her anger on Tanya overcame the tears. "She's in my theater class. And she's a Junior Demonette, a member of the drill team. You know, those girls who wear cutesy little costumes that hardly cover their butts and do cutesy little routines, all in a long line. Kicks and so on." Pazit flopped down again on the chaise and raked her hair out of her eyes.

Ellen made another swoop through the salsa

over Brian's head. "Too bad he's already got a girl-friend. But it would still be nice if you had a friend like him in the band, to give you some support."

"Forget it," Pazit said, too loud, on the brink of losing it. Ellen just could not seem to shut up. "I don't need support. Especially not his."

"Pazit, we have to discuss this band thing," her father said gently. "The ACLU takes this stuff very seriously. They want to make a legal case of this. The local chapter has already called in the regional director, and they've consulted a lawyer. They intend to try to force your Mr. Dalrymple to stop marching in a cross and to make up a program that isn't exclusively religious music. Yesterday Mrs. Lovett called to tell me the ACLU director and their attorney are meeting with the principal of your school and the band director tomorrow morn-ing. If Mr. Dalrymple won't change his program voluntarily, then I think the ACLU might take him to court."

Pazit was on her feet in a flash. "Dad, you promised!" she wailed. "You promised you wouldn't do anything unless we talked it over! And now look what's happening! They're going to make a big federal case out of it, and everybody will know it's me, and I might as well be dead as go back to that school!"

"Maybe not," Ellen said soothingly. "There

have probably been some other people complaining, don't you think?"

"No, I don't think!" Pazit was trembling, and tears of anger and frustration rolled down her face. "I'm the only one! Don't you understand that? *The only one!*"

"Maybe it won't be as bad as you think, *mi hijita*," her father said. "Maybe Mr. Dalrymple will show that he's a reasonable man, and he'll work out a new routine that will be even better than the one he's got. I can't for the life of me figure why anybody with good sense would want to have a cross at a football game. And the kids will see how important this issue is. It could be a great learning experience for them—they could see how the Constitution operates to protect everyone." He looked at her affectionately through the thick glasses that had slipped down on the bridge of his nose. "I know you don't care about any of that. I don't blame you. They gave me their word you wouldn't be brought into this in any way. You know I'd do anything to keep you from getting hurt, *mi hijita*."

"But you don't understand, Dad!" She was screaming now. "You don't understand anything! Everybody will *know* who complained. I'm the only one in the whole school that doesn't like it, the only one that's said anything. And that . . . that

Billy you think is so neat, he's just as bad as all the rest of them. He won't even *speak* to me!" Pazit collapsed sobbing onto the chaise.

Her father laid down his barbecue tools and sat down beside her and pulled her onto his lap the way he used to when she was a little girl, stroking her hair. "I'm sorry, Pazit," he murmured. "I didn't realize how bad it was for you here."

Her mother picked exactly that moment for her Sunday call. Pazit blew her nose and picked up the phone.

"How's school?" Ruth asked. "You've started?"

"Yes, Mom. Tuesday. It's all right."

"What courses are you taking?"

"Algebra," Pazit said. "Language Arts. Government. Biology. Dad wants me to take Spanish but I'm taking theater." Then she added, "And I'm in the band."

"Your father's right about Spanish. It's important to have another language. Theater can wait. Are they regular classes, or did you get in advanced placement?"

"Regular, Mom. I didn't try for A.P."

Her mother started to say something and then seemed to change her mind. "Rosh Hashanah starts Wednesday the fifteenth of September," she said abruptly. "Are you coming home?"

Pazit had avoided thinking about the High Holy Days until now. "I don't know," she said evasively. "I'd have to miss school."

"Suddenly you're worried about missing school!" Ruth snapped. "That's a new one." But then her tone softened. "Talk it over with your father," she said. "You know I would like you to come."

"I know," Pazit said, her voice choked with yearning for a life different from the one she had.

PAZIT WAITED UNTIL her father had turned out the light in his study and gone downstairs to bed before she tiptoed into his study and called Rachel for the third time this week. Since the start of school and the problem with the band, there had been a lot to talk about.

"Hey, how's it going?" Rachel asked. "Have you got them marching in a Mogen David yet?"

Pazit laughed. "No, but I'm working on it." She loved that idea: a Star of David cruising down the field while they played "Havah Nagilah." Not in a million billion years would that ever happen in Jericho!

The laughter turned to a hard lump in her throat. "Oh, Rachel, you can't believe how awful it is here! In biology class on Friday the teacher was talking about 'Mr. Darwin's so-called theory of evolution,' like it was something very peculiar, and then she said, 'Of course we all know that the true story of the Creation is found in the Book of Genesis, although we're required to teach Mr. Darwin's theory as well.' So I raised my hand and said I thought evolution had been the accepted theory for years and years, and she stared at me and said, 'PAY-zit'—that's what she still calls me—'PAY-zit, I'm sure you'll find that a great many people of the Jewish faith also accept the Old Testament description of the Creation of the world and reject the heathen interpretation of Mr. Darwin.' " Pazit mimicked Mrs. Farnham's accent almost perfectly, a trick she had learned from her father.

"Oh, God," Rachel sighed. "Did you get into it with her?"

"Why bother?" Pazit said. "But there's more. One of the guys in the class was wearing a T-shirt that said 'Over billions of years single-celled organisms evolved into man,' with a picture of a squiggly cell and an arrow pointing to an ape, and then an arrow from the ape to the man. And at the bottom in huge red letters it said 'NOT!' Followed by a whole paragraph of small print explaining how it was God who made us, et cetera, et cetera. And everybody was admiring this guy's stupid shirt."

"Wow," Rachel murmured sympathetically. "It must be like the Stone Age there."

"It is."

"You need to come back to Denver."

Pazit sighed. "I don't know. Mom wants me to come for Rosh Hashanah."

"Oh, that would be so great! Are you coming?"

"I don't know. I'm thinking about it."

"So, listen," Rachel said, "what about that kid, Billy, you were telling me about? Have you seen him?"

"Yeah. I saw him. He probably thinks we're all descended from Adam and Eve, too. I wouldn't be surprised if he's got a shirt just like the one I saw."

PART THREE

Marching

Whispers

MONDAY MORNING, bleary eyed, Pazit tossed a banana into the blender with milk and a dash of cinnamon. She also checked the fridge for bagels. Sometimes Ellen bought her the frozen kind, which would have to do, since you obviously couldn't get fresh ones here in Jericho. The two she found were hard as rocks, and she put them back.

The family was already in gear. Her father, up since five as always, was drinking coffee and looking over the *Jericho Advocate,* "For signs of intelligent life," he said. Ellen concentrated on getting the little guys ready for school. This was another thing that Pazit found annoying about this family—they were all morning people except her. She was like her mother, who loved to stay up late and sleep in. Her father's early morning cheerfulness drove Pazit crazy.

"Good luck, sweetheart," Gus said, getting up to give her a huge hug as she prepared to leave. "If anything happens today, and I don't know that it will, but if anyone says anything to you, just hold your head up and remember that you are in the right! OK?"

"Right," she sighed.

"Hang in there," Ellen said.

Walking to school as the sun crept over the treetops and the temperature began to rise, Pazit wondered if anybody would be on her side after all—possibly one of the teachers, although she couldn't think who—or if she really would be all alone. The worst of it was, she wasn't even *on* a side! She just didn't want to march in their stupid cross.

She managed to get to the practice field exactly on time, neither early nor late, and took up her position on the sidelines with her flute.

"Band!"

"Sir!"

Mr. Dalrymple paced back and forth, dithering over every little thing. "Here's a note that has to be played," he rasped over his field mike, "and it has to be played *right!* And not only *right,* but with energy! With confidence!"

They repeated those notes several more times, but nothing seemed to satisfy him. A half hour passed. Sweat dripped. There had been no rain since the storm that brought Tripper, and a layer of powdery dust rose in a thick cloud and stuck to her skin. Pazit's throat was dry, but her plastic canteen of drinking water stood forgotten at home on the kitchen counter.

"Halt!" snapped the director.

Pazit stifled a nervous yawn and waited warily to see what was going to happen next. Suddenly Mr. Dalrymple stopped his restless pacing and gazed out at the band. He looked haggard.

"There's something I have to tell you," he said, his voice hoarse and ragged, almost shaky.

Here it comes, she thought, squinting through the haze of dust.

"We've got a problem. All of us do. I'm sure y'all remember what's happening a week from this Friday night?"

"Opening game!" they all roared. Pazit braced herself for whatever was coming.

"That's right. Only a week and a half—eleven days, people!—until the opening game, when every eye will once again be upon the Pride of Demon

Country." Everybody hollered, "Yaaay," but Mr. Dalrymple signaled for silence. "Eleven days until we show the world once again that we are the best. But it's my sad duty to tell you that something very serious has happened." Every eye was on Mr. Dalrymple. Nobody moved. Pazit felt light-headed and wished she could sit down. "It could come to pass," he said, "that we may not perform the program we've been rehearsing day in and day out for the past few weeks, that we started planning last spring."

"*Whaaat?*" The question rumbled through the band. Suddenly Pazit was afraid. She wanted to run before he said anything more, but she concentrated on standing absolutely still. She stared straight ahead, listening to the thump of the pulse in her head.

"It seems that some unknown person, some cowardly person who has chosen to remain anonymous, has complained to the American Civil Liberties Union that we are in violation of the Constitution of the United States."

She could hear the sneer in his voice. She felt like screaming, "It's not my fault! I didn't want to do this. I didn't want to ruin your program, and I'm sorry that's what's happening." But they wouldn't believe her.

"This person claims that his or her First Amendment rights have been violated by our program of religious music. Particularly by our marching cross, the highlight of our routine. Yes! Ladies and gentlemen, believe it or not, we are lawbreakers!"

Pazit guessed from the quick glances that everyone in the band had figured out she was responsible. She heard their excited murmurs and knew they were talking about her. She could feel their outrage boiling up. Their anger scared her, and she tried to calm herself with slow, steady breaths.

The drum major called out, "What are we going to do, sir?"

Mr. Dalrymple shook his head. "I don't know yet. I just found out about this last night. I'll be meeting with our principal and some members of the school board and I guess some of those ACLU people later today. I intend to stand up for our rights, people. I promise to do everything in my power to make sure that one or two malcontents don't spoil the hopes and dreams of all of you who have worked so hard for so long." His voice cracked. "That will be all for this morning. Band dismissed!" Head lowered, he hurried off the field.

They looked at one another, stunned, and then everybody began to talk at once. A couple of the girls started to cry. One of the clarinetists ran up to the drum major, who nodded and blew his whistle.

People stopped talking to listen. "We're going to pray," the drum major announced.

Immediately band members reached out to hold hands with each other until they were all joined in a continuous chain. They bowed their heads. "Our Father," the drum major began, and everybody chimed in, "Who art in Heaven."

Pazit hurried toward the school, her head throbbing. She knew that even with their heads down, they were watching her. She tried not to run.

Later, on her way to her first period class, she passed a group of girls from the band and looked the other way. They made sure she heard what they said: "Jew bitch." Just those two words, repeated twice, so she couldn't miss them.

The rest of the morning was not much different from any other: Pazit walked alone to classes, sat stonily while the teacher asked questions that other people answered halfheartedly. At lunch she ate her slice of double-cheese pizza by herself. No one spoke to her. No one looked at her—at least not directly. She felt them staring and imagined them whispering as word spread rapidly through the school:

"The band's halftime program might be scrapped . . ."
"It was her fault, you know, that new girl . . ."
"The band can't march at the game next Friday . . ."

"She bitched to somebody, said she wouldn't march in a cross so nobody else could, can you imagine?"

"The band's out of the district competition, they don't have a chance if they have to change the program . . ."

"She's a Jew, you know."

"Jew bitch . . . Jew bitch!"

THERE WAS NO way she could go to fourth period band. Right after lunch, her stomach began to heave. She barely made it to the girls' rest room in time.

"How you feel otherwise?" Mrs. Wells, the school nurse, inquired later, feeling for her pulse.

"A little shaky," Pazit confessed, relieved to be in this quiet place, grateful for the nurse's cool touch on her wrist.

"You want me to call your mama to come get you?" Mrs. Wells, who was black and plump and comfortable-looking as a feather pillow, examined Pazit through large, round glasses that magnified her brown eyes.

Pazit shook her head. "I'll be OK," she said. "Just an upset stomach, is all."

"Up to you," the nurse said, guiding her to a narrow white cot in the next room. "You lie down for a few minutes till you're feeling like yourself again. I'll be right here if you need me." She tucked a cotton blanket around Pazit and left her alone.

Pazit closed her eyes and tried to doze. But when the bell rang at the end of fourth period, Pazit crawled off the hard cot and collected her books.

"You sure you're OK now?" Mrs. Wells inquired.

"I'm fine. Thank you." Only study hall, algebra, and theater class, and then she could get out of this place; three more periods and she was free.

It was obvious that everyone knew. The students in study hall either stared at her openly or ignored her, as they had all along, but now she sensed that anger had taken the place of curiosity. In algebra there was a lot of whispering and nudging, but the teacher pretended nothing was happening. The minutes ticked by. There was a sub in theater class, and he read them a play, taking all the roles himself. When the dismissal bell rang after what seemed like hours, Pazit fled for home, weeping with hurt and anger.

Troublemaker

THE HARPERS WERE saying grace when the phone rang again. It had been ringing practically nonstop since Billy got home from school. If it wasn't for Brenda, it was for their mother.

"Enough is enough. Let the answering machine get it, Brenny," Mr. Harper said. "You know the rule."

The rule was that they were not allowed to take any phone calls while they were eating supper. Mr. Harper, especially, was real strict about that. This rule was meant to apply particularly to Brenda, "the social butterfly," as Dad called her. Chuck, her boyfriend, had learned never to phone during supper; mostly the calls had to do with Demonettes or with Teen Disciples, of which Brenda was vice president. The phone was hardly ever for Billy. When it rang, he just kept on eating.

But before the machine could click on, Billy's mother leaped up and grabbed the phone. His father stopped with his forkful of Monday night chicken halfway to his mouth and stared at her. "Virginia?"

"*This one* is important, Rich," she said, muffling the receiver against her chest.

Billy's dad nodded. "All right, we'll wait," he said, and put his fork down.

BILLY HAD BEEN wondering all day, since Mr. Dalrymple's incredible announcement this morning, what was going on. And he had been thinking about Pazit.

Billy had watched her rush off the field. She looked so small and forlorn, and so alone. He didn't understand any of it. Pazit hadn't said anything about this, but then he hadn't really talked to her since before school started. Well, he'd tried. He'd called, and she'd blown him off. He'd looked for her when he went to mow their lawn on Saturday, but she hadn't come out.

That morning when they'd finished the Lord's Prayer, Chuck had added a few lines of his own. "Jesus, we ask you to bless this band and Mr. Dalrymple and make sure we get to play our music and perform our marching routine just the way it is, for your glory. Amen."

"Amen!" the band responded. They squeezed hands before letting go and started drifting back to the school in little groups, buzzing about what had happened.

Billy had fallen into step with Twig Terwilliger, who looked as though the world had just caved in on him. "You don't think they'll keep us from marching, do you?" Twig asked. His lip trembled as though he was about to cry.

Billy shrugged. "I guess they could."

A bunch of girls sped by, their voices shrill and angry. "It was that Jew bitch," he heard one of them say, and Billy sucked in his breath.

"You think it was?" Twig asked. "You think it was Pizza who did it?"

"Pazit," Billy said.

"What?"

"It's pronounced *pah-ZEET*."

"She a friend of yours or something?"

Twig had looked straight at him, demanding an answer. Billy hesitated for only a second. Then he shook his head. "No," he said.

He'd felt kind of bad for saying that. But when he thought of what she had done and how it was affecting all these people, he truly believed what he had told Twig: Pazit Trujillo was no friend of his.

During fourth period Mr. Dalrymple's assistant, Mr. Fisher, explained that the director was tied up in a meeting. He had them march in place in the band room while they played through their program.

"Mr. Dalrymple expects to see all of you out on the field tomorrow morning as usual," Mr. Fisher said. "He may have more to tell you at that time."

A couple of people had waved their hands and tried to ask questions, but Mr. Fisher just shook his head. "I don't know any more than you do," he'd said.

By the end of school there were plenty of rumors, but no real facts. And the telephone wires had been burning up.

"THAT WAS FRANK McBrayer," Mrs. Harper announced, sitting down again, a little breathless. "He wants me to activate the Band Boosters' telephone tree. We're going to get as many people as possible to come out to the school-board meeting tomorrow night and speak in support of Mr. Dalrymple and the band."

Mr. Harper frowned and looked at Billy sharply. "Tell us what you know about all this, son."

"I guess there's somebody who doesn't like the cross formation," Billy said, doing his best to blank Pazit's face out of his mind. "And they're trying to get it stopped. Mr. Dalrymple said this morning they went to the American Civil Something Union and complained."

His father stabbed a french fry. "You're sure about this? Somebody's gone to the ACLU?"

"That's what Mr. Dalrymple told us this morning. And he wasn't in fourth period band class. So I don't know what's happening."

"I know all about those people. Bunch of communists. They ought to call themselves the Anti-Christian Losers Union," Mr. Harper said with a snort.

"You know what else I heard?" Brenda put in. "It's some Jewish girl who doesn't like it. Billy knows her, right, Billy?"

Billy felt his face heating up. "Uh-huh." He reached for a slice of bread.

"Who is she, honey?" his mother asked.

"A new kid. A freshman. She just moved here this summer, and she joined the band. She plays flute. That's all I know." Billy spread margarine on his bread with extreme care.

"Is she Jewish?"

"I guess so."

"Where from?"

"Denver. But she used to go to school in Israel." He immediately wished he hadn't said that. The more he told them, the more they would question him.

"Let me get this straight, Billy," Mr. Harper said, peering at him hard. "This Jewish girl moves here from Denver or Israel or wherever, she joins the band as a freshman, and the first thing she does is tell the band director he has to change his entire program because she doesn't like it?" He let out a bark of laughter.

"Something like that," Billy mumbled. A blob of ketchup had dribbled on his dad's shirt.

"And Mr. Dalrymple is actually taking this girl seriously?"

"He said it has something to do with the Constitution," Billy said, barely above a whisper. "I don't understand it either."

"She's a little troublemaker," Brenda put in. "You can tell that just by looking at her."

"How can you tell that, sweetie?" Mrs. Harper asked. She had a very small portion of chicken and a big serving of salad, iceberg lettuce and low-cal dressing. Billy's mother and sister were always on some diet. Maybe his mom needed to trim off a few pounds, but Brenda didn't. Brenda had a fear of fatness. If she gained so much as an ounce, she'd lose her chance of ever becoming a cheerleader for the Dallas Cowboys, which was her big dream.

"She dresses real weird," Brenda said.

"Like what?"

"Oh, some kind of baggy pants and long, draggy skirts and lacy sweaters you can see her underwear through. She doesn't shave her armpits. I guess that's the way they dress in Israel, but it looks *real* strange here."

At least, Billy thought, his sister hadn't mentioned the toe ring. It was a wonder Tanya hadn't found out about the armpits.

"That doesn't sound so weird," Mr. Harper said. "I'd be happier if my daughter wore baggy pants and long skirts than some of the outfits she does come up with."

"Dad!"

Billy roused himself. "I don't think she looks like a troublemaker. I think she looks like a normal person who isn't from around here and dresses different," he said.

"But she *is* a troublemaker," Brenda insisted. "Just look what she's doing! Mrs. Sheffield even said this afternoon at drill team practice that if the band can't play, then maybe we won't be able to do our routine either. I mean, who is that girl to cause all this to happen? She's just one person! And if she doesn't like it, so what? This is a democracy, after all! Why doesn't she just shut up and go back to Israel if a Christian cross bothers her so much?"

Mr. Harper crumpled his paper napkin into a ball and dropped it on his plate. "What we need to do before we do anything else," Mr. Harper said, "is pray. After all, that's what this is all about, isn't it? Our right to worship Jesus the way we always have?"

The Harpers joined hands around the kitchen table, and Billy bowed his head and listened to his father's prayer. "Lord Jesus, we ask you to be with us in this time of trial, in which our faith is being tested by the infidels of this world. We ask you to strengthen us against the Antichrist and to remind those who would oppose us that you are indeed Lord over all. Amen."

"Amen," Billy said automatically. The phone rang almost immediately. It was for Brenda.

Monday night was Bowling League. Billy's dad collected his shoes and ball and team jacket and got ready to leave for the alleys, where he bowled with the men from the hardware store where he worked. Mrs. Harper bowled with the bank team, but she called her captain and said she couldn't make it because of an emergency. Of course she told her the whole story.

Then Brenda announced that she was going to start calling to get the Demonettes together at school the next day to pray about the band problem. She decided to go to her friend Holly's house and do her phoning from there.

Billy couldn't decide what to do with himself. He kept wondering about Pazit. Did she have a clue about the effect all this was having? He remembered how lonely and scared she looked and figured she didn't. Maybe he ought to warn her that she'd just lit the fuse to a bomb that was about to go off with a huge bang. His parents and his sister believed Pazit knew exactly what she was doing. Billy didn't know Pazit real well, but he didn't think she had planned it to turn out this way.

Maybe if she realized what was happening, she'd change her mind and tell this ACLU to forget she had said anything. Then they could all go back to the way it was before. They'd march in their routine, play their songs, entertain the people who came to watch, and win the trophies. That's all it was supposed to be about. It wasn't supposed to be about anybody's *rights,* for heaven's sake.

Billy got a few quarters out of his Car Jar, dropped them in his pocket, mouthed "I'll be back soon" to his mother who was on the phone telling somebody else about "the troublemaker," and rode his bicycle three blocks to a convenience store with an outdoor phone booth.

He dialed Pazit's number. Her father answered. "Is Pazit there?" Billy asked.

"Yes, she is, but would you mind calling back in about an hour? Or could she call you later? I'm on the phone right now on some important business, and—"

"That's OK," Billy said. "Never mind." He hung up. Everybody was on the phone this evening. Mr. Trujillo was probably calling people at the ACLU, urging them to keep the band from doing its program.

Billy started to ride home, but changed his mind and veered in the opposite direction: downtown. It was still early, his mother would be on the phone for hours, his father and sister weren't at home. He could easily ride to Pazit's house, ring her doorbell, inform her of what was going on so she could tell her parents and they'd call the whole thing off, and then he'd ride home again. That would put an end to the whole business, wouldn't it?

But suppose it didn't. Suppose Pazit really was dead set against the marching cross, not only for herself but for the whole band, and she intended to fight for her constitutional rights, whatever that meant. He'd feel like a real fool then.

He didn't know what to do. He felt sorry for her. But she was *asking* for trouble, even if she wasn't *making* it.

Before he had even crossed Pioneer Boulevard, the boundary between his part of town and hers,

Billy abruptly changed his mind a second time and swung up a curving side street toward Shawn Stovall's house. Maybe if he came right out and told Shawn about it, he could get his own head screwed on straight.

Shawn's sister, Cara, came to the door. Cara was a sophomore and played baritone sax in the band. Billy had always thought Cara was a pest, but when she took up bari sax, her whole personality seemed to change, and she began to act very cool.

"Hey," Cara said when she saw Billy. "Here's Mr. Wonderful. You came to see me, right?"

Billy, embarrassed, shook his head.

"Well, go on up, then. You know where he is," she said, pretending to pout.

Mrs. Stovall stuck her head out of the kitchen. "I was just talking to your mom on the phone, Billy."

"Tell her I'm here, will you please? If you talk to her again?"

"Hey, Harper," Shawn said when Billy gave their secret knock, *da-da-da-dah,* Beethoven's Fifth. Billy let himself into Shawn's room, which was bathed in an eerie glow. Shawn was hunched in front of his computer, as usual. "What's up?"

"Not much," Billy lied.

"My mom's going nuts over this band thing," Shawn said. "Is yours?"

"Yeah."

"Everybody I know is coming completely unglued. Twig was actually bawling this morning right after the Colonel made his announcement. So what's your opinion? You think there's anything we can do?"

"I don't know," Billy said. "I wish there *was* something we could do."

"You think it was Pizza True Jello?" Shawn asked. "It seems like she's trying to get things stirred up."

Billy shrugged. "I don't know," he said again. "I feel kind of sorry for her. Her name's pronounced *pah-ZEET,*" he added.

Shawn looked at him curiously. "Man, I'd stay away from her if I was you," Shawn said. "However she says her name, she's pure poison. You don't want *nothin'* to do with her."

Billy tried to swallow, but there didn't seem to be a drop of spit in his mouth. "I was thinking of going to talk to her," Billy said. "See if maybe she'd want to change her mind, if she knew how upset everybody was."

"Oh, come off it! She'd just make you look like a fool, I bet. You ought to come right out and challenge her in front of everybody. Show her she can't just come here and start pushing people around."

Well, I guess that answers that question, Billy thought. "Forget it," he said. "Not my style." He stood up and stretched. "Gotta go."

"Hang on, I'll walk you outside." Shawn followed him down the stairs and out the front door. Billy could hear Mrs. Stovall talking a mile a minute on the phone in the kitchen. "I put your name in today for student council," Shawn said.

"You did? First I heard about it."

"Well, it's not like we didn't talk about it. I think you'd be good. You know, 'The Voice of the Little People.' I'll be your campaign manager."

"*What* little people are you talking about?"

"Me. Twig. Lots of people."

"Twig? He's not so little. In fact he's huge."

"I don't mean *physically.* I mean guys who aren't jocks or whatever it takes to be Mr. Popularity."

"How about girls? Little girls, too?"

"Of *course* I mean girls. That's the whole point, man. Showing the girls we're on their side. That you don't got to be a big handsome dude in a football jersey to be lovable."

"Sort of a nerd ticket."

"No! Jeez, Harper, what's gotten into you lately? It's not like you don't have one of the prettiest, nicest girls in the whole school for your girlfriend." He chuckled. "And that dumb sister of mine would change places with Tanya in a heart-beat. She's even offered to make posters for your campaign."

Billy squinted at Shawn in the darkness. He hadn't realized Shawn thought so much of Tanya. And he didn't think he *wanted* to know that Cara thought so much of *him*. Billy reached out and punched Shawn lightly, affectionately, on the arm. "OK," he said. "You be my campaign manager. Now I really gotta go."

"And stay away from the Jew-girl, all right? I can't get you elected if you hang around with weird types."

Billy started to say that she wasn't weird, but he shut his mouth. "Catch ya later," he said and headed home. It was too late to go down to talk to Pazit now anyway.

His mother was off the phone and waiting for him when he got home. She followed him into his room, which was unusual. He braced himself for the same old lecture on cleaning up his room. She always made it sound like it was one of the Ten Commandments, or maybe the Eleventh: *Thou shalt keep thy room neat, and any room in which thou spendest time, like the TV room.* But this time she didn't seem to notice that he still hadn't put away his laundry from last week.

"Billy," she said. "There's something I want you to do."

"I was just going to do it," he said automatically.

She shook her head. "I don't mean your room. I mean I want you to come to the school-board meeting with me tomorrow night."

He nodded. *Boring,* he thought. He wasn't surprised that she'd want him to go, show his support for Mr. Dalrymple and all. Probably a lot of band kids would be there with their parents.

"And I want you to get up and say how you feel about all this."

"In front of everybody?" he yelped. "You want me to talk in front of all those people?"

She nodded calmly. "That's exactly what I want you to do. I was talking to folks from Band Boosters this evening, and we agreed that it needs to come from the kids in the band as well as from the parents. Mr. McBrayer is going to talk, because he's the president. I'm planning to say something. And I volunteered you."

"But why *me?*" Billy demanded. "All those other parents in Boosters, they've got kids in the band too, don't they? And every one of them can do it better than me."

"Because you always come across as very honest

and sincere, Billy, and that's what counts. Remember when you stood up in church and gave that report after church camp last summer? Everybody told me afterward how good you were, because you just came right out and said what was in your heart. And that's what I want you to do tomorrow night. Not from your head. You're right—anybody can do that. From your *heart*, Billy!"

When his mother had gone and left him alone, Billy lay on his bed and thought about it. He tried praying, too: *Help me, Jesus.* But it was hours before he fell asleep, and he still didn't know what, exactly, was in his heart, except an awful lot of confusion.

Strolling

"Can you believe it, Pazit?" Ellen said, laughing. "Obviously the woman who called had no idea who she was talking to. She asked if I was Mrs. Trujillo, and I said yes—easier than explaining the maiden-name business—and next, did I have a daughter in the band, and I said yes to that, too. I still didn't know what this was about, understand. Then she told me she was calling for Band Boosters to tell me that everybody's getting together at the school-board meeting tonight to show support of Mr. Dalrymple and the band, and could I possibly be there on such short notice? And of course I told her I certainly could."

"You're going?" Pazit asked incredulously. "You're going in support of Mr. Dalrymple?"

"Well *hardly,* but she doesn't know that. I'm going mostly out of curiosity, to see for myself what this bunch is really like and what they have to say for themselves. I might even get up there and speak for our side." Ellen was fishing a handful of soggy teabags out of the jug of sun tea. "The problem is, I'd love to have you come with me, but your dad has to teach a class tonight and I'd like you to stay home with the kids, if you don't mind. I won't be gone long. I'm just going to buzz over there, see what's going on, and come right home."

"Sure," Pazit said. She let out a sigh of relief. For a minute she'd been afraid Ellen would try to talk her into coming along to the meeting, and there was no way she was going to do that. There'd be band kids, and they'd see her, and it would make everything worse. If it could *get* any worse.

Tuesday nights were rushed because Gus taught an evening class. He and Ellen watched the early local news and weather report and the first part of the national news with Tom Brokaw, and then Ellen had an early supper ready because Gus had to leave by six-thirty. But it wasn't too rushed for Gus to ask Pazit for a report on school.

"So how did it go today, *mi hijita?*" he asked. They were eating chicken salad made from the chickens Ellen had roasted the night before. It looked like a dairy-free zone, and Pazit was hungry. She hadn't been able to swallow even a mouthful of her double-cheese pizza at lunch.

"Mr. Dalrymple said this morning at band practice that he intends to fight, whatever the ACLU decides to do. He says the ACLU wants to stamp out all signs of religion and make this a godless country. He says the band is within its rights to play anything they want to, and since they're only playing the tunes and not singing the words of the hymns, that doesn't count. But he says he's afraid they're going to force him to change the cross, and if he has to do that, the band may not have anything in good enough shape to win the regional competition. And when he said that, everybody started making the worst racket you ever heard, just *blasting* on their instruments, like one gigantic razzberry."

"And where were you during all this?" Ellen asked.

"Standing there on the sidelines, like an idiot."

"Oh, Pazit! It sounds just awful for you! Did anybody say anything to you?"

"Well, by now everybody knows I'm Jewish. That's not exactly a secret."

"And? What does that mean? Did something happen?" her father asked. "You know, Pazit, if I had known it was going to get like this, I wouldn't have called the ACLU. I'm not sure what I'd have done, but I never intended anything like this."

"It's kind of late to think of that now!" she exclaimed.

"What happened, Pazit?" Gus insisted.

She had decided not to tell them about the girl who'd hissed *"Jew bitch"* yesterday in the hall. Somehow she felt that if she didn't talk about it, then it hadn't happened: she hadn't heard it, and they hadn't said it. But again today, in the hall between classes, she'd heard it again, a low, snaky sound: *"Jew bitch."* She had been careful not to react. *Don't give them any satisfaction,* she'd told herself, keeping her eyes straight ahead. And she didn't tell her parents now either.

"Nothing," she answered Gus. "Nothing happened."

There was the usual rush as her father collected his books and papers. Then Ellen decided to change her clothes for the school-board meeting. "Everybody dresses up for everything here," she complained. "Back in the Springs I hardly ever put on stockings and heels. Here, they get dressed up to go to the dentist." She came out in a jeans skirt and a white shirt with a turquoise necklace and her Mexican sandals. "Do I look respectable?" Ellen asked, striking a pose for Gus.

"You look gorgeous," Gus said approvingly, but he always said that. Her father was not a good judge of style, in Pazit's opinion, but Ellen hadn't asked *her*. "Now don't do anything radical, all right?" he warned Ellen.

"Who me?" Ellen asked with fake-innocent eyes, and they both laughed.

"You'll be OK here with the boys?" Gus asked Pazit on his way out after Ellen had gone.

"We'll be fine," Pazit promised, her arms around Brian and Matt. They all waved as their father backed out of the driveway.

"Tell you what, guys," she said when he had beeped once and driven off, "let's take Tripper for an evening stroll. We'll stop at Sadie's for a treat. And when we come back, you can help me clean up the kitchen, OK? How does that sound?"

"Yeah, yeah!" Matt crowed.

"What's a stroll?" Brian asked.

They snapped on Tripper's leash and headed for the courthouse square. Strolling had become fairly strenuous, because Tripper was getting bigger and stronger and towed them in his wake as he lunged from one bush to the next, raising his leg and marking at each stop. Pazit yanked on the leash to get him past a couple of cats, who stretched themselves into defiant arches, and one enraged Yorkshire terrier chained to a porch post. They stopped to peer in the window of a taxidermist's shop, where a stuffed black bear snarled out at them, and a hardware store with a display of antique tools that none of them could identify.

The little guys loved Sadie's. Gus had discovered the diner where he could sit by the hour and nurse a cup of coffee and read, and then he started bringing the whole family there as a special treat on Saturday mornings for breakfast. Pazit checked her pockets to be sure she had enough money to buy them all ice-cream bars.

"I'll stay out here with Tripper," she said, handing them each a dollar. "Bring me an ice-cream sandwich. Chocolate." Then she remembered that only an hour had passed since she'd had the chicken salad; it was much too soon to eat dairy. "Wait—make that a bag of barbecued chips."

While the kids were in Sadie's, Pazit stood outside with the dog, watching the evening traffic cruise slowly around the square that bloomed with bright yellow and orange flowers. The boys dashed out of Sadie's with their ice-cream bars and Pazit's bag of chips. As they waited for the walk light, a blue Chevy drove by. Staring out of the window was Billy Harper. He seemed to be looking right at her, but when Pazit raised her hand and waved, Billy turned away.

Public Speaking

"WE'RE GOING TO be late," Mrs. Harper fumed. "I thought I'd made it clear to Brenda that if she uses the car, she's got to make sure there's some gas left in the tank."

They had barely made it to the filling station. Billy pumped the gas because his mother didn't want to mess up her good silk dress and because he liked to do it anyway, pretending it was his own car he was gassing up. Then, in spite of being late, his mother had driven at exactly the speed limit all the way downtown to the Education Administration Building.

Usually her extremely conservative driving style drove Billy crazy, but this evening he was just as happy to be late. He did not want to go to this meeting. Seeing Pazit with Tripper and her little brothers in front of Sadie's finished it. When she waved, he turned his head away and slouched down in his seat.

"You know that girl?" his mother asked.

"Sort of. She's from school."

"How come you didn't wave back when she waved to you?"

"I don't know. Didn't feel like it, I guess."

Mrs. Harper drove around the block twice, looking for a parking space. When they were locking the car, Billy thought of telling his mother he'd meet her later and then taking off to look for Pazit over by the courthouse. He needed to talk to her, to let her know that none of this was his fault. But instead Billy followed his mother into the administration building. She worked her way through the noisy hallway and into the auditorium. Every seat was taken, and lots of people were standing.

Most of the people there were adults, but Billy spied some band kids. Shawn and Twig were jammed up against the opposite wall. The members of the school board sat up on the stage at a long table. A camera crew from Channel 6 News panned the crowd.

A bronze-haired lady bustled up and down the

aisle with a handful of yellow cards, calling out, "Any more? Any more?"

Billy's mother flagged her down, got two blank cards, and handed one to Billy. "Put your name on here, plus your age and also that you're a band member. We got here just in time."

The chairman banged his gavel, calling for order, and asked for the invocation. A man in a black suit stood up and said, "Let us pray." Immediately the room hushed. Billy bowed his head and whispered a prayer of his own. "Jesus," Billy prayed, "help me do right. Please. Amen."

The bronze-haired lady gathered everybody who wanted to speak and lined them up in the order in which she had collected their yellow cards. Numbly Billy got in line next to his mother. "All right," said the man with the gavel, "we'll now hear from the public. Please step up to the podium, give us your name, and make your statement, limited to three minutes."

The first person up was Mr. McBrayer, president of the Band Boosters. "I've come to speak out in support of our wonderful band and especially our dedicated band director. Let's give a big ovation to Mr. Paul Dalrymple, who is standing at the back of the room, and let him know what we think of him."

Everybody turned around and gawked. Mr. Dalrymple waved briefly, and everybody stood up and clapped hard. A few of the kids whistled. The TV crew zoomed in on him, and the flashgun of a newspaper reporter's camera blanched the director's face white.

When everyone who had a seat sat down again, Mr. McBrayer continued. "My question to all of you is: Who's right? Ninety-five teenagers who have worked hard for weeks to prepare a magnificent program? Or one discontented outsider who comes here and starts complaining and insisting on rights? Whose rights are being violated?—that's what I want somebody to tell me."

Chuck Johnson made his way to the podium. As drum major he sometimes intimidated Billy, but without his uniform and tall red shako with the white plume, Chuck looked like an ordinary guy—just his sister's boyfriend. "The ACLU says if we play Christian hymns, then we're promoting Christianity, which is against the law. My question is, if we play music written by Tchaikovsky or some other Russian, does that mean we're in favor of communism? If the composer happens to be homosexual, does that make it look like we're promoting a gay lifestyle?"

More applause.

Now why did they clap for that? Billy wondered,

watching the drum major leave the podium with a satisfied smile. *It didn't even make sense.*

For the first time Billy noticed Mrs. Trujillo way down the line ahead of him, waiting for her turn. He almost didn't recognize her, all dressed up. What was she doing here? He moved back so she couldn't look right at him and smile or say, "Hi, Billy," or something that would make his mother ask questions.

The pastor of Billy's church stepped up to tell the crowd that it was not the band's program but the name of Jesus that was causing the controversy. "The presence of Jesus Christ Almighty is making the Devil uncomfortable!" he thundered. If it hadn't been for the three-minute limit, Billy thought, he'd probably launch into one of his sermons. "Let us not allow our children to fall victims to this vicious attempt to eradicate religion from their lives!"

Next was Mrs. Evans, Tanya's mother. "Excellence is not achieved easily," she began, reading from a paper. She described how hard the kids had worked, which Billy agreed with, and how they deserved to be allowed to perform their program, no matter what. The kids cheered, and Billy said, "Yeah!"

Shawn Stovall's dad took the microphone. Billy could sense excitement growing in the crowd, the mood rising. "Whatever happened to freedom of speech?" Mr. Stovall demanded. "This is censorship, pure and simple," he said. "This is a democracy, based on majority rule. But our young people are being told to stop doing the program they've trained for and the program they want. It's *their* rights that are being trampled! We have a moral obligation to these wonderful children of ours to protect their rights." A roar of approval.

Pazit's stepmother walked to the microphone. "I'm Ellen Scanlon," she said, "and I've come to speak for the other side." A murmur swept through the crowded room. "I find it odd that a band director in a public school would plan a program consisting entirely of religious music, music representing only one of the great religions of the world," she continued in a shaky voice. "But I wouldn't have come here except for the issue of the marching cross. Marching in the form of a cross while playing Christian music is illegal in a public school. I think you all know it's illegal."

Some of the band kids started to mutter out loud, drowning her out. The gavel pounded and she tried again, her voice faltering. "You talk about the rights of your children. But what about the rights of the child who is not a Christian? Whatever happened to making room for everybody? Even those who disagree with you." Ellen Scanlon stepped back from the podium.

For a moment there was dead silence as she walked away. People moved aside to let her through. "Who is that woman, anyway?" Billy's mother asked right out loud. There was no applause, only the sound of hissing like a snake slithering through the crowd. Billy hoped Mrs. Trujillo didn't hear the ugly sound, the same way he hoped Pazit didn't hear the ugly things kids were saying about her at school. *Whatever happened to making room for everybody?* echoed in his ears.

A few more adults came forward to say something about freedom of religion and freedom of speech. Ashleigh Reynolds, Twig's girlfriend, talked about how important the band was to her, and how much she admired Mr. Dalrymple for everything he did, and then she started to cry and couldn't go on.

Billy kept hoping somebody else might speak up in support of Pazit and her stepmother, although he couldn't think of anybody who would. Nobody he knew agreed with them.

As the distance shrank between him and the head of the line, Billy got more nervous. "Mom, I don't want to do this," he whispered.

"Do it anyway," she whispered back. "Other

kids are doing it. Ashleigh did it. Just talk about how you feel, Billy. It's not so important what you say as how you say it," she coached him. "The important thing is to show that we're all behind Mr. Dalrymple and the band, and that one screwed-up person is not going to ruin it for everybody else."

Billy wiped his sweaty palms on his pants. Trouble was, he didn't think Pazit was screwed up. Different, was all—unusual. He liked it that she was different and unusual. Most of the time in his life Billy had been pretty much like everybody else. He had always tried to fit in. Everyone he knew had grown up the same way he had, believing in the same kind of things. He had never questioned any of that . . . until he met Pazit.

Pazit must be feeling real bad, Billy thought, *knowing everybody is against her.* He could imagine how he'd feel if somebody tried to make him do something in a religion he didn't believe in—kneel on a rug and face east or something. Maybe he'd do it and maybe he wouldn't, but he'd hate it. She probably hated this, too. She was just doing what she thought was right—and *not* doing what she thought was wrong. She'd probably been brought up that way, the same as he was. "The easy thing," his dad always said, "is to go along with the crowd. The hard thing is to stand alone and do what's right."

The line moved forward again. He tried to think what he was going to say, but his brain was a jumble. Maybe the chairman would decide this had been going on long enough and cut it off. And at that moment the man with the gavel did announce that they would have time for only three more speakers. Billy was the third. His mother, in line ahead of him, beamed him a bright smile.

"Let somebody else take my place, Mom. Please!" he begged. "I don't know what to say."

"The Lord will tell you what to say. Just the way He's helping me." She patted his arm and stepped confidently up to the microphone. "Ladies and gentlemen," she began, "my name is Virginia Harper, and I'm here to tell you how proud I am of the band and all its members. My son is in that band, and so I know firsthand how hard those kids have worked and how important it is to them to be able to perform what they've been trained to perform. I don't want to see my son, or your son or daughter, cheated out of the opportunity he deserves. What kind of message are we giving our children when we tell them that *one unhappy person* can take away everything they've earned? I say, let's support our kids and keep 'em marching straight, the way they've been taught!"

Billy scarcely heard what his mother had to say, but he did hear the clapping. Smiling broadly, she gave him a quick hug as he stumbled toward the podium. A minute ago his mind was a jumble and now it was blank. He ran his dry tongue over his dry lips and looked out at the crowd. *Jesus help me,* he prayed again. *Tell me what to say.* He bent down a little to speak into the microphone. From somewhere his father's voice echoed in his mind: "Do what's right," and then his mother's, "The way you've been taught."

"I think," he croaked, "that the person who doesn't want to march in a cross is right, if it's against her religion. I wouldn't want to either. And if we all can't do it, then maybe we shouldn't have the cross at all."

He hadn't known that's what he was going to say, or even what he thought, until he got up there and opened his mouth, and that's what came out. He walked away from the podium. He saw his mother staring at him, her mouth open. He'd done it now.

No one applauded, but no one hissed, either, at least not that Billy could hear. His ears were buzzing, so he couldn't be sure. He had to get outside for some air. But as he stumbled toward the exit door at the rear of the auditorium, he saw Mrs. Trujillo, or whatever she called herself, standing apart from the rest. She looked straight at Billy, unsmiling, and winked.

"Good for you, Billy," she whispered as he passed her. "You've got guts."

Billy sat on the curb by his mother's car, his head in his hands. This, he thought, had been the worst night of his life. *Guts?* He wasn't so sure about that. All heck was going to break loose, he could bet on that. Everybody would come down on him, and he probably hadn't done Pazit a bit of good anyway.

''I HAVE NEVER, *ever* been so embarrassed in my life," his mother said in a trembling voice as they drove home. "My own son gets up in front of everybody and says what you said. 'Maybe we shouldn't have the cross at all.' Isn't that what you said, Billy? Did I hear you right?"

"Yes, ma'am," Billy muttered. "That's pretty much what I said." They were driving up Fourth Street, past the yellow brick house with the bright blue door. Billy glanced up at the window in the gable under the peaked roof. The light was on. He wondered if that was Pazit's window. He thought of her standing on the corner of the courthouse square with her dog and her little brothers, before he had spoken in front of all those people. It seemed like hours and hours ago.

"Wait till your father hears about this, that's all I can say," his mother said, so angry she was almost choking on her words. She hardly ever got this mad. "Making a fool of me like that."

"I don't see how that made a fool of you," he said softly. "I didn't want to talk. You told me the Lord would tell me what to say."

"And you're telling me that He told you to contradict me in public? Seems to me it's more like the Devil putting words in your mouth!"

"Anyway I forgot to say my name. I was too nervous. So probably nobody even knows that you're my mother. It's not like I said, 'I'm Billy Harper, that lady's son.'"

"Billy, there really must be something wrong with you. Everybody knows I'm your mother! They saw me hug you on your way up to the podium! What must they be thinking? You made everything I had just said seem false."

It was a mistake to argue with her. Billy knew that. He struggled either to make himself shut up or else to agree with her and apologize, and he lost both struggles. "But I still think she's right," he said. "She's not a troublemaker. She's just sticking up for her rights."

"*Her* rights? Why are you so worried about *her* rights? What about the rights of everybody else? What about Mr. Dalrymple's rights? What about the rights of all the kids in the band who've worked their hearts out and then are told that some outsider can come in and tell them it was all for nothing, nothing at all?"

"She's not an outsider. She lives here. Her parents live here."

His mother's driving had become more aggressive. She had raced through a yellow light at Pioneer Boulevard, honked at a car that was taking too long to make a left on Vermont Street, and then coasted through the stop sign a block from their house, something that always made her mad when other drivers did it.

"And who is this *person* the rest of us have to change everything for? Is she a *friend* of yours, Billy?"

"No, ma'am. I've just talked to her a couple of times."

Billy thought of the day Pazit had crashed through the bushes chasing Tripper into the Shoemakers' yard. And of the day they'd built the doghouse. It seemed liked months ago. He remembered how Shawn had asked him the same question: *Is she a friend of yours?* Twig, the same thing. He'd told them *no*, too. Told everybody *no*, like he'd been afraid to admit the truth. But now he stopped feeling afraid.

"Actually," he said, "that's not true. She *is* a friend of mine."

His mother drove into the garage, stopping

barely an inch from his father's workbench, and yanked on the emergency brake. The space where his dad parked his truck was empty. Billy was relieved not to have to face him right away, but it was not going to be good when he did get home. His mom would tell his dad the whole story, and no matter what Billy said, he could already see how his father's face would darken and the heavy lines around his mouth would deepen. Then it would begin: Richie would never have done anything like this, never let the family down, never made his mother look bad.

They were barely in the house when the phone rang. It was Tanya. "Billy Harper," she wailed, "I just do not see how it is *possible* that you could stand up in front of the whole *world* and say what you said! Who told you to say that you think that awful girl is right?"

"Nobody told me," he replied. "It's just what I felt. What I feel," he corrected himself.

"But don't you see what that *means?*" she said, her voice clogged with tears. "If the band doesn't play, then the drill team doesn't get to perform."

"Well, I don't think—"

"Of course you don't think! That's obvious, Billy, that you don't *think.* You just go right ahead and open your mouth, and whatever comes out is fine with you! Because you don't care about anybody else's feelings. I felt so sorry for your mom, because she just looked like her heart was about to *break* when you said what you did. And what about *me?* I guess you don't care one bit for me, either, do you? My mom got up and talked, but you probably don't even remember what she said, or else it doesn't matter. Because all you care about is that girl with the flute, that terrible girl who my daddy says is probably a radical of some kind, trying to demolish Christianity."

"OK," Billy said wearily. "I guess we can talk about it some other time."

"Don't count on it, Billy," Tanya warned. "Because as of right now, I'm not speaking to you!" The phone crashed in his ear.

Brenda leaned in the kitchen doorway, her face unreadable. "You done with the phone?" she asked.

"Yeah." He tried to catch her eye, but she looked away. "I suppose you heard about it, too?"

"Just what Mom told me, but she wasn't making a lot of sense. What did you *do,* Billy?"

"All I said was, I thought the person who doesn't want to march in a cross is right if it's against her religion, and maybe we shouldn't have the cross if it bothers some people. That's all."

Now Brenda looked at him incredulously. "That's *all?* Isn't that *enough,* Billy? I can't believe my own brother would stand up in front of a whole crowd of people and say something like that! Doesn't your religion mean *anything* to you, that you can't defend it? That you'll let some . . . some *Jew* tell you what you can and can't do? And how do you think it makes the rest of your family look? Did you think about that for one second? I mean, I'm the lieutenant of the Demonettes, and how do you think it looks when my own brother—"

The phone jangled again, interrupting her. "You answer it," he said. "It's probably for you anyway. Or Mom."

But it was Shawn Stovall for Billy. Brenda thrust the phone into his hands and stomped off.

"Thanks a lot, buddy," Shawn said bitterly. "I thought we were friends."

"We are," Billy said. Was this going to go on all night?

"Like heck. I can't believe you said what I heard you say. I mean, after I take the trouble to put your name up for student council, and I'm ready to go all out and get you elected, then you pull a deal like this. Traitor! You know? That's what it feels like to me. After all we been through together, and you sell the band down the river, like it means nothing at all."

"All right," Billy said. He covered his eyes with his hand. "All right."

Headlines

"WELL, YOU DID IT, you two," Gus said. "You made headlines." He spread the front page of the *Jericho Advocate* on the table, among bowls, cereal boxes, milk carton, juice glasses, and coffee mugs.

Pazit stopped peeling a banana and leaned past him to look. Centered on the front page was a big photograph of the band taken from high above the stadium during one of their halftime performances, probably last year's. Over the ninety-six identical white caps the headline blared the news:

SCHOOL BAND ROUTINE
THREATENED BY SUIT

To the right was a column headed:

Hundreds Turn Out,
Support Bandleader

Gleefully Pazit's father read the lead article aloud, describing the action proposed by the ACLU to prevent the band from performing its religious routine. There were interviews with the principal of the school, the head of the school board, and the board's attorney.

"They sound like knuckleheads," Gus said. "Why did they let that guy Dalrymple get away with this in the first place? Doesn't anybody at that school pay attention to what's going on?"

Ellen was more interested in the story about the people who attended the school-board meeting. There was a photograph of Mr. Dalrymple with a half smile, one hand raised. "He looks positively beatific," Gus said. "Like the Infant of Prague." Mr. McBrayer was quoted, along with some others who spoke in support of the band director. There was no mention of Ellen.

"Hardly what you'd call balanced reporting," Gus said. Then he came to the paragraph quoting Chuck Johnson: "If we play music by Tchaikovsky, does that mean we favor communism?" and Gus burst out laughing.

172

"They left out the part about homosexuals," Ellen said drily. "After the bit about communism, the kid said something like, 'if the composer is homosexual, does that mean the band is in favor of being gay.'"

Gus was cracking up. "Give me a break! Did he actually say that?"

"He did. Gus, believe me, it was like being in a strange country. I've never felt so out of place in my life."

"That's how I feel," Pazit said. "All the time."

Gus and Ellen stopped chuckling at the newspaper articles and looked at her. "I know," her dad said sympathetically. "And it may not get better for a while, *mi hijita.* All you can do is stick it out until it eventually blows over."

"But you *don't* know," Pazit insisted. "You have no idea what it's like. I'm completely alone there! I feel like I'm from another planet!"

"Not completely," Ellen said. "You've got your friend Billy."

"Oh *Billy,*" Pazit said, dismissing the idea. "The nerd."

"Hey, wait a minute, Pazit. That 'nerd' spoke out last night in your favor. You should have heard him."

"Billy spoke?" Pazit asked. "*Against* the band?"

She found that hard to believe. She couldn't imagine him speaking against anybody.

"You bet he spoke," Ellen said, "but not so much against the band as for *you*. I was very impressed. It couldn't have been easy for him, because a lot of his friends were there, plus his mother. That 'nerd' has a lot of integrity. I wish you had been there to see and hear. No, on second thought, I don't. It would have gotten to you, Pazit, I'm afraid. It sure got to me. I wasn't prepared. One after another, people getting up and defending that band director and his ridiculous program, claiming everything from God's will to the right of majority rule, everybody clapping and cheering for whatever nonsense came out of somebody's mouth. And then I went up and spoke my piece. I was quaking in my shoes, let me tell you! And when I finished they started going *sssssss*. That's never happened to me in my entire life! But the incredible thing was Billy. With all the know-nothings who went up there to talk, Billy was the only person who made any sense at all."

"What did he *say* exactly?"

" 'The person who doesn't want to march in a cross is right,' and then something like, 'if we all can't do it, then maybe we shouldn't have the cross.' Words to that effect."

"Did people hiss at him?"

"No, oddly enough. I think they were too surprised because they expected him to say something else. They were just very, very quiet. I was going to get out of there after I had my little say, but I'm glad I stuck around. I wouldn't have missed that for anything."

Everything in her life took strange turns, Pazit felt, but this was more bizarre than usual. "Gotta go," Pazit said around a mouthful of banana. "Be late."

"For band practice?" Ellen asked.

Pazit swallowed. "Yeah." She saw Gus and Ellen look at each other.

"You're still going to go? After what's happened? Are you sure that's a good idea?"

She grabbed her book bag and started for the door. "I've got a right to play. I'm just not going to march."

"It's raining," Ellen pointed out. "Pouring, in fact. They don't practice outside in the rain, do they?"

"If there's thunder, they go inside." She rummaged in the hall closet. "Have you seen my rain poncho?"

Ellen delved into the closet and found the poncho. "But don't the instruments get wet? I mean, don't the horns fill up with water or something?"

"It's not raining *that* hard." She wrestled the

175

plastic sheet over her head. It nearly reached the floor.

"You look like a ghost!" chortled Matt.

"Boo!" Pazit said, flapping her arms.

Gus laid down his newspaper. "Sweetheart, I think this is going to be tougher than you think. Maybe it would be better if you'd just forget about the band for a while. Let the ACLU handle it."

"Let the ACLU handle it!" she exploded. "That's why it's the mess it is now, because of the ACLU!"

"No, it was a mess before that. It's been a mess from the beginning. You had no way of knowing what you were getting into. But now you know. And nobody would think badly of you if you decided to quit."

Pazit made a sour face. "They're not going to force me out. Period. Here I go. Wish me luck."

"Stubborn," her father said, shaking his head. Then he hugged her, poncho and all, and kissed her above each eyebrow. "*Nolite te bastardes carborundorum.* That's Latin—sort of. It means, 'Don't let the bastards grind you down.' "

Traitor

I CAN'T BELIEVE you said that!

Billy had heard it now from just about everybody. His mother and father. Tanya. Brenda. Shawn. Twig. Heard it in every tone of voice—anger, disappointment, dismay. And he didn't really have an answer for any of them, except that's what he felt, deep down: *I think she's right.*

"Band!"

"Sir!"

Mud splattered Billy's white high-tops, but he didn't much care. He felt less exposed blanketed in his plastic raincoat, even though it was like being inside a greenhouse. He kept the hood pulled up, cutting off most of his side vision so he didn't have to see what kind of dirty looks he was getting from everybody. But that didn't stop him from *feeling* their anger. The telephone wires must have been humming all over town last night, as the band members who were at the school-board meeting called the ones who weren't and told them how Billy Harper turned traitor.

Billy was astonished to see Pazit standing on the sidelines, buried inside a rain poncho and playing her flute just like nothing had happened. This morning, surrounded by band members who all probably believed he was just as bad as she was, Billy had a pretty good idea of what she must be feeling. And it hurt.

As usual Mr. Dalrymple had them play through their music first, no marching, to make sure the notes were in their heads, so much part of them that they didn't have to think which note came next. That was the way he liked to warm them up. Then Mr. Dalrymple turned on his field mike and made an announcement.

"First, I want to thank all of you who came out last evening to support the band at the school-board meeting. We were definitely the majority—in fact it was almost unanimous in support of our program." Billy's face burned and he chewed his lip. "Now, a progress report. At eleven o'clock this morning I'm meeting with the lawyers for the school and for the ACLU to find out what they've worked out. They're coming down hard on us, people, make no mistake about that. The powers of evil thrive in Jericho! I hope I'll have good news for you fourth period, but I'm warning you now, we may have to make a lot of changes. I'll do my best, but we may not win this one.

"It's possible," he went on, while Billy shifted miserably from one foot to the other, "that we won't get to do our routine the way it should be done, and we won't get to play the music exactly the way it should be played. And so I'm making a special request. I'm asking you to go through our program now and to do it perfectly. This could be the last time."

The last time? Billy blinked back tears. He stood with his drumsticks ready. Out of the corner of his eye he saw Pazit with her flute poised. The drum major gave the downbeat, and the band—minus Pazit—stepped out to the opening bars of "Amazing Grace."

And it *was* pretty amazing, Billy thought, after they had executed the last of the quick moves that set them up for the cross formation. The tempo shifted, and they segued into "A Mighty Fortress Is Our God," beginning their majestic kick step across the field, the snares filling in the long beats with a snappy tattoo, Twig Terwilliger's cymbals clashing dramatically.

They came to a halt in front of the Colonel, perched high on his portable stand. "That was perfect," Mr. Dalrymple said after a moment, his voice choked with feeling. Billy could not think of a time he had ever heard that from the band director. "I will always remember this. Thank you."

The drum major blew his whistle, the signal to dismiss. The rain had stopped. Slowly the members of the band sloshed across from the muddy field, little groups of two or three or four huddling together. Billy walked alone. He paused for a second and glanced at Pazit, wiping off her flute. She looked back at him, her dark eyes wide. He kept on going. *Later,* he told himself, *I'll talk to her later.*

Nobody spoke to him for the rest of the morning. He wouldn't have noticed, except that Shawn and Twig seemed to go out of their way to avoid him. He decided not to go to the cafeteria for lunch; his stomach felt like somebody had tied it in a bow. He thought about cutting fourth period, except that he felt drawn to the band room, to find out what was happening. His stomach growled all through Mr. Dalrymple's announcement.

"A compromise has been worked out, people. It's not one I like, and it's not one you're going to like either, but it seemed better than to throw out everything. Here's what we agreed to: we'll keep two of our pieces, 'Amazing Grace' and 'Precious Lord, Take My Hand,' because I managed to convince them that these are jazz versions popularized by secular musicians and therefore aren't really 'religious.' We'll replace 'Onward Christian Soldiers' with a piece we did last year that I think we can get up to speed pretty fast. And I'm planning to rearrange 'A Mighty Fortress' so that even Martin Luther himself wouldn't recognize it, but you'll catch on quick."

"What about the cross, Mr. Dalrymple?" Chuck Johnson asked.

"Well, that's the crux of it, isn't it?" Mr. Dalrymple forced a thin, tight smile. "There won't be any cross. The ACLU lawyer threatened to get an injunction to stop us from marching at all if we kept the cross. I'm sorry. I had no choice. I'm going back to the drawing board to work out a new marching routine by tomorrow. That gives us a week and a day."

"All because of that awful girl!" Michelle Simmons, first trumpet, spat out. Billy glanced toward the flute section, but Pazit's chair was empty.

"But what are we going to *do?*" someone wailed.

"The best we can," Mr. Dalrymple said. "Just

remember, the Lord is on our side." Then he pretended to catch himself: "Oops! Guess I'm not allowed to say that around here anymore, am I?"

KNOWING THAT IT was useless, Billy waited by Tanya's locker at the end of school.

"What do you want?" she demanded, glaring at him.

He shrugged. "I thought maybe we could talk."

"There's nothing to talk about. I told you, after what you did, I'm not speaking to you. Now if you don't mind getting out of my way—"

"OK," he said. But, as he watched her leave, Billy realized he didn't care if Tanya was speaking to him or not.

Threats and Promises

"YOU HERE AGAIN, Pazit?" Mrs. Wells asked. "That stomach still giving you fits?"

"I guess so."

"You been to see a doctor?"

"No. I didn't feel sick after last time. I thought I was OK."

"Huh! Maybe yes, maybe no. Let's check your temperature."

Pazit settled onto the wooden chair next to Mrs. Wells's desk and let the nurse slip the thermometer into her mouth and reach again for her pulse. Mrs. Wells checked the thermometer, shook her head, and jotted something on a small yellow pad. Then she leaned back, folded her arms across her broad bosom, and looked Pazit over carefully.

"Boyfriend got eyes for somebody else? Algebra test you don't want to take? What's *your* diagnosis? Because you came to see me fourth period a couple days ago with an upset stomach, and by fifth period you're fine, and now here it is fourth period again and here *you* are again. So I think maybe you know more about what's bothering your insides than you let on."

Pazit didn't know what to say. If Mrs. Wells thought her upset stomach was a made-up story just to get out of something, she was wrong. Pazit hadn't invented the stomach cramps or the nausea or the lunch she had just lost in the girls' rest room again. She gazed down at the cracked floor tiles, trying to pull together an answer.

"What class you got fourth period?" Mrs. Wells prodded. "Let's start with that."

"Band," Pazit whispered.

"Band? Marching band, you mean?"

Pazit nodded. Mrs. Wells was probably a Christian. She probably thought like everyone else around here that it was all right to have a marching cross in a public high school, even if she was too nice and polite to say so. Maybe she even had a T-shirt saying evolution didn't happen.

"So what's your problem with the marching band?"

184

"I'm the one," Pazit began, and then her mouth went dry. She stopped and began again. "I'm the one that started the whole thing about the cross," she said. "I'm Jewish. I can't march in that cross because I don't believe in it, and my parents say it's illegal anyway."

"Uh-oh," Mrs. Wells said.

Pazit waited, but that was all the nurse said: *Uh-oh.*

"So I went to practice this morning, out on the field."

"In the rain?"

"Yes. And Mr. Dalrymple told us he'd find out this morning what's going to happen. If they're going to make him change the formation and play different songs or what. And since this morning might have been the last time the band would get to do the routine they wanted to do or to play the music they wanted to play, he asked them to perform it just once, perfectly."

"And what happened?"

"It was the best they ever did it. Before, somebody was always screwing up something. This morning, no mistakes at all."

"Where were you all this while?"

"Standing on the sidelines, playing. Mr. Dalrymple said I could still play, if I wanted to."

"But why you want to do a thing like that?"

185

Mrs. Wells asked, a frown rippling her smooth, dark face. "Be apart from everybody else?"

"Because I'd be apart anyway," Pazit said softly. "And I like to play."

Mrs. Wells shook her head sadly. "All I got to say is, no *wonder* you got a bellyache. I heard about some of these goings-on, to be honest with you, and I thought maybe you were some kind of trouble-maker. But I see I was wrong about that. Now I'm not going to tell you you're right about this, and I'm not going to tell you you're wrong, either. But I am going to tell you any time you feel the need, you come on in here and sit a minute or two with me, and we'll talk, or not talk, depending. Maybe it helps your stomach to know you got one friend here. All right?"

"Yes. Thank you."

"Now you rest yourself a little, and I'll fill out an excuse form, and when you feel up to it, you be on your way."

Pazit curled up on the white cot and shut her eyes, picturing the band as it moved precisely through the moves of the cross routine, ninety-five people, perfectly synchronized. If they performed that way in competition, they'd win. No question.

She also saw again the way ninety-five people deliberately turned away from her. No—ninety-

four. Billy had looked at her, just for a second. And then he'd turned away, too.

Pazit stayed on the cot in the nurse's room until the last bell rang. She hadn't intended to be there the whole time, but somehow she couldn't bring herself to leave this safe place.

Before she left school, she stopped by her locker to pick up her rain poncho and her flute. Out fell a sheet of lined yellow paper that had been folded up and crammed through one of the vent slits in the locker door. Pazit unfolded the paper and read:

> *This is a Christian town and a Christian school, and if you don't like the way we do things, too bad. Now that you ruined everything, don't bother showing up to practice anymore. Why don't you go back where you came from? No one wants you here.*
> *P.S. - Your ugly black dog might suddenly get sick if you keep on with this stuff.*

Pazit crumpled the paper, stuffed it deep in her book bag, and rushed out into the warm gray drizzle.

She found Billy at the bike stands, bent over his dripping bike lock. "Hey," she said.

He looked up. "Hey."

"I was wondering," she said, "if you'd walk home with me."

Billy yanked on the lock and stood up, towering over her. "Sure," said Billy. "Let's go."

WHILE BILLY WHEELED his bike beside her, hardly saying a word, Pazit thought about the yellow paper wadded up in the bottom of her book bag. Who could have written that note? Almost everybody in the school was some Christian telling her to go away. But how many of them knew about Tripper? And who would be mean enough to threaten to harm her dog?

Billy might know who wrote it. It might even be a friend of his, like that big oaf with the cymbals, or the other bass drummer. She would have suspected Tanya, but the note said, "don't bother showing up to practice anymore," and Tanya wasn't in the band so that seemed to eliminate her. That still left ninety-some other possibilities.

They waited for the light to change at Davis Drive. All the traffic lights glowed in the mist. "Do you think I'm weird?" Pazit asked suddenly.

"Not exactly weird," he said.

"What does *that* mean? Yes or no?"

The light turned green and they hurried across, Billy's bike splashing through puddles.

"Depends," Billy said. "Mostly I just think you're different."

"Different *how?*"

"Well, for one thing, asking questions like that! And to be honest, the way you dress isn't like the girls here. You don't even *look* like girls around here. I knew the first time I saw you that you were from someplace else. I thought you were a foreigner. You know that toe ring you wear?"

"My toe ring?" It made her laugh, and that felt good. She hadn't laughed in days. "I keep telling people I'm from Denver, I was born there, but I guess they don't believe me."

"Not with that toe ring, they sure don't."

By the time they'd reached her house, Pazit still hadn't told him about the note, and she *had* to find out who had written it. "You want to come in?" she asked.

Billy looked uncomfortable, as though he couldn't decide. "Well," he said finally, "OK, but just for a few minutes. I have to get home pretty soon. It's Wednesday."

"Yeah, it's Wednesday. So?"

"Wednesday is church night. Most people around here go to church Wednesday night. I belong to Teen Disciples, the youth group at our church, and me and my sister go to that while our parents are in the Prayer and Praise Group."

Pazit had never heard of anything like this. "And you think *I'm* different and foreign and strange? *Whooo-ee!* I don't think I ever met a Teen Disciple who went to church every Wednesday night. Come on in for five minutes," she said. "I've got something to show you. You won't be late, I promise." Then she added under her breath, "Watch out for Ellen. You're her Hero of the Week."

She wished her stepmother would back off, but Ellen seemed overjoyed to see Billy and immediately leaped into her Good Stepmother role, getting out cookies and juice for them as though they were little kids. "Can I offer you anything else? A sandwich or something?"

"This'll be just fine, ma'am," Billy said politely.

"Let's take this stuff and go out on the patio," Pazit said, dropping the package of cookies in her book bag.

Billy and Ellen both looked at her. "But isn't it awfully wet out there?" Ellen asked.

"Not really. The rain is nice. And we could sit under the umbrella."

Billy shrugged. "If that's what you want to do."

Water puddled in the plastic patio chairs, but Pazit dumped it out and sat down. Tripper barked a couple of times for attention until Pazit hollered at him to be quiet. He retreated into his blue house and lay watching them.

Pazit ripped open the package of cookies and poured the juice. "Ellen's all right," she explained, "but there's no privacy. It's better out here."

"That's OK," Billy said, gobbling up a handful of cookies. "I don't mind."

"Listen, Billy," Pazit said in a low voice. "There's something I want to show you, and I don't want her to know about it. Or my dad, either. Or anybody. Promise you won't tell?"

When he'd promised, she dug out the yellow paper, unfolded it, and smoothed it out on her knee before she handed it over to Billy. "Be careful not to get it wet."

She watched Billy's face while he read the note. He glanced up at her once, frowned, and read it again.

"So what do you think?" she asked.

"I think it's awful," he said. "I think whoever wrote it is sick. And I think it's terrible that some-one did this to you."

"Do you have any idea who wrote it?"

Billy shook his head. "No, I sure don't."

"You don't recognize the handwriting or anything?"

"Nope. But listen—how many people know about your dog? It has to be somebody who knows you have a dog."

Her hands had started to tremble slightly, and she folded them to keep them still. "I walk him around the neighborhood, is all." Pazit took the note from Billy, folded it carefully, and tucked it back in her bag. "I'm wondering," she said, "if we could do some kind of handwriting analysis. You know, if you'd somehow get hold of samples of handwriting from everybody in the band, then we'd compare."

"You're talking about ninety-four people, Pazit. I wouldn't know how to do something like that."

She thought Billy seemed nervous, and she got the sudden idea that maybe he really did know who had written the note and was protecting somebody. "I was hoping you'd help me. I guess nobody's ever threatened your dog or told you you're not welcome and you ought to get out of town. It never happened to me before, either. I hope if it ever happens to you, somebody is willing to help you."

She could taste the anger in her voice, but she couldn't seem to control it. All of her anger gathered itself together and focused on Billy. If Billy didn't get out of there, *right now,* she thought she might start to cry or leap up and dump a glass of cranberry juice all over him.

But when she saw the look on his face— stunned by her outburst, and hurt—she felt ashamed of herself. Billy Harper was probably her one and only friend in this stupid town, he had actually had the nerve to stand up and defend her at a big meeting, and now she was treating him as though he was one of *them*.

"I'm sorry," she said, really meaning it. "You've already been helping me. Thanks for saying what you did at the meeting last night. Ellen told me about it. What made you do that, anyway?"

Billy gazed at the cookie package, now half empty. "It just seemed like somebody had to say something," he said with a shrug. "My mom made me go to the meeting, and she said it was important for me to get up and make a statement. I didn't want to do it. But I got tired of everybody talking like there's only one side to it, and all the good people are on that side and everybody else is completely wrong. So I just said what I thought was right."

"Ellen thinks you're the one person in this town with integrity. That's what she calls it—integrity. I didn't plan for it to turn out like this, Billy. I didn't *plan* anything! I just didn't think I should have to march in that cross, since I'm not Christian—as everybody and her great-grandmother knows by now. But I didn't know the cross routine was against the Constitution or the Bill of Rights or whatever until I mentioned it to Dad and Ellen, and then the whole thing went ballistic."

"Maybe you ought to tell your folks about that note, Pazit. People can do some real strange things."

"Do you think anybody would actually come here and hurt Tripper?" Her voice was calm, but inside she was shaking.

"Well, no, I don't think so. Whoever wrote the note was probably just trying to scare you, to get you upset, so you'd quit. You're not from around here, you're new, so maybe you don't understand how important this is to everybody in this town. Here in Jericho, you go to church on Sunday, you go to church on Wednesday night, and on Friday night you go to the high-school football game. Football is almost like religion, like church. Life is real simple here, I guess. That's what my family's done forever. My sister, Brenda—do you know her? Tall and blond? She's on the drill team."

"Everybody here is tall and blond," Pazit said sourly. "Now you've got one person in Jericho

High School who's short and dark. No, I don't think I know her."

"Anyway, she's lieutenant of the drill team. And my dad played tackle for Jericho High School when he was a student, and my brother, Richie, was quarterback and even got a football scholarship to Tech. My mother played in the band at her school in Manasseh. Everybody we know has pretty much the same story. That's why they're so upset, I guess—the grown-ups the same as the kids— because football is such a big thing in everybody's life, and the band is part of football."

"Oh, I get it," Pazit said drily. "Band is as important as football is as important as church. But here's what I don't get: if church is so important, why are people who go to church so nasty? The preachers on TV are always talking about *luuuv*. But love isn't what this is about. This is about trying to scare me into doing what they want by threatening to hurt my dog."

"I don't know, Pazit. I can't explain it."

She reached for another cookie and realized there weren't any. "I'm sorry," Billy said. "I didn't mean to eat up all the cookies."

"It's OK. To tell you the truth, I've been so upset lately my stomach is really messed up."

"Mine, too. I didn't eat lunch."

"I lost mine," she said. "I threw up."

"Oh." Billy made a face. "At least I didn't barf. I just couldn't eat."

"You couldn't?" It was hard to believe that Billy would be troubled, too. He always seemed to fit right in, to be part of the group. Not an outsider like her.

"You know something?" Billy said. "I think the band is making you sick."

"Maybe it's making you sick, too, Billy."

"Yeah." He grinned and shook his head. "What a thing to have in common."

"Listen," Pazit said. "Let's go inside and get some real food. Then we'll bring it out here, OK?"

Eluding Ellen, they grabbed crackers, a slab of cheese, a jar of peanut butter, a knife, and a couple of apples and took them outside. Pazit cut the apples in quarters and began slicing the cheese. Maybe she was being too hard on him, Pazit thought, expecting him to turn into a private investigator. "Do you have any ideas, besides telling my parents, what to do about this note?" she asked.

"I'm thinking about it. I'll come up with something. But meantime I've got another idea. There's something else I want to do." Billy leaned toward her. "You know that shirt you had on the other day?"

"Shirt? What shirt are you talking about?"

"It has the Jewish star and a bunch of Jewish writing on it. I was wondering if I could borrow it for a couple of days?"

"What for?"

"To wear."

"To *wear?* You want to wear one of my shirts?" Pazit had a sudden rush of panic; was this some boy-girl thing they did here, swapping shirts? Because if this was a hint that he was *interested* in her, there was no way. She eyed him suspiciously. "Why?"

"To show all those people who are against you that you're not all by yourself, you're not totally alone. That you've got somebody on your side. A friend. That's what I want to be."

She hesitated only a second. "OK," she said. "Wait."

Pazit ran upstairs to her room. It was a disaster: bed unmade, clothing scattered everywhere, drawers hanging half open, closet door gaping. She plowed through the mess, snatching up handfuls of clothes and pitching them into a corner. Eventually she unearthed the shirt Billy wanted, in the bottom of the laundry basket. At least it was clean. She spread it on the bed and tried to smooth out the wrinkles. Then she took it downstairs.

"You kids still don't have sense enough to come in out of the rain?" Ellen called out from her studio.

"It's nice," Pazit insisted, rushing through the kitchen. "Refreshing."

Billy had gone over to Tripper's pen, and Tripper was engaged in his favorite sport, grabbing his rawhide bone and running in frantic circles. "He's a real nice dog," Billy said. Tripper bounded over to the fence to be petted. "I can't imagine anybody would try to hurt him."

She handed Billy the shirt. "I don't know why you're doing this, but if you want to wear it, here it is."

"You told me what the writing means, but I forgot," Billy said.

"*Shalom aleichem*. It's Hebrew. It means 'Peace be with you.'" That's what Leon had called to her when she left Israel. Ninety-five days ago.

Billy folded the shirt and stuck it in the saddlebag of his bike. "Maybe I'll wear this tonight to Teen Disciples. See what happens."

"Good luck," Pazit said. "*Shalom aleichem*."

"*Shalom aleichem*," Billy called as he wheeled his bike out to the street. He even pronounced it right.

Mogen David

BILLY TRIED ON the shirt. It was a large and hung on Pazit like a tent, almost to her knees, but it fit Billy fine. He thought it looked pretty good. He tried to imagine how it would be when people saw him in it—his parents shocked, the youth pastor surprised, his friends upset, the rest of the band mad as heck. Nobody would understand what he was trying to do. Nobody would understand that he was just trying to stick up for a person who had nobody else to stick up for her.

Billy peeled off the shirt and stuffed it, wrong-side out, in the bottom of his underwear drawer. It didn't seem like the right time to wear it. Not yet.

He went downstairs and unloaded the dishwasher, set the table with plastic placemats, plates, and silverware, and put the rest of the dishes away. He cranked open two large cans of barbecue beans and dumped the contents in a saucepan. Next he opened a package of hot dogs, slit each frank down the center, and stuffed the franks with strips of American cheese.

Then he wrapped strips of bacon around each cheese-stuffed frank, fastened the bacon with toothpicks, and lined up the franks on a broiler rack. He wondered what Pazit would think of his cooking, but he knew he'd probably never find out. Pazit wouldn't be welcome in *this* house.

Billy thought of the shirt in his bottom drawer. He could forget about Tanya forever if he showed up wearing that shirt. Tanya hadn't been in his mind at all when he asked Pazit to lend him the shirt. Now he thought about her, her face pink with anger, her hands clenched in tight little fists, her voice high, loud, screeching. They'd had a few fights—*fusses,* his mother called them—but they hadn't been about anything real important. Not like this.

He found the package of hot-dog buns, spread margarine on six of them for himself and his dad, left two plain for Brenda and his mom. Most of their fusses, he thought, had to do with Tanya being jealous. Sometimes she got jealous of other girls. If she caught him at what she called flirting and he called just being average friendly, she always got over it. "I forgive you," she'd say, as though he really had done something wrong and she was being big-hearted.

He shredded up some iceberg lettuce in a salad bowl, checked the refrigerator bin for ripe tomatoes, chucked a rotten cucumber in the garbage.

Tanya's complaints about Shawn were different. She didn't like Billy spending so much time with Shawn, time she thought belonged to her. "I have friends, too, Billy," she'd told him, "but I never let them come between you and me. I wouldn't do that. But I guess you have a different idea about things."

Well, yes, he guessed he did have a different idea, but it wasn't worth fighting over. He kept quiet about when he was spending time with Shawn, which he thought wasn't any of Tanya's business anyhow. "The only thing that should ever come ahead of me is family," Tanya announced, like she had just read it in the Bible. "If you really loved me, Billy, it wouldn't be a problem for you."

Given her attitude, it was clear to Billy that there was no way he could spend any time at all with Pazit without Tanya getting upset. But she had already announced she wasn't speaking to him, since his two or three sentences in front of the school board that seemed to have doomed him to an exile he was only just beginning to comprehend.

He set the paper-napkin holder in the middle of the table along with jars of mustard and relish, and a set of salt and pepper shakers in the shape of cactus. He got out four glasses for iced tea.

"If you really loved me, Billy . . ." But *did* he really love Tanya? He wasn't sure he knew what love was all about. He liked her a lot, he thought she was pretty, he felt good when he was with her, and he liked the idea that she liked *him.* But was that love? They had been going together for what seemed like a long time. Everybody thought of them as a couple, and almost everybody at Jericho High School was half of a couple. His mom liked the idea that he was going with a girl from a good family, although his dad thought maybe they were a little too good—living out by the country club and driving a Lincoln.

He found a package of mix for pineapple upside-down cake in the cabinet and decided to fix it as a surprise. He followed the directions to the letter, put the cake in the oven, set the timer, and cleaned up the mixing bowls.

As he was doing this, he thought about Pazit. He liked her a lot. He thought she was pretty— not pretty like Tanya, but pretty like herself. It felt good to be with her. He'd enjoyed building the doghouse, and this afternoon sitting out on her backyard patio in the rain while she told him about getting sick in school and showed him the note, he realized that his feelings went a lot deeper than liking. Deeper than whatever it was he felt for Tanya.

The day he wore Pazit's Star of David shirt, that would be the end of Tanya, no question. And of all the others—they were still plenty upset with him. It would be real hard to face them, most of all Shawn. Of all the people who were mad at him for what he'd said at the school-board meeting, Shawn hurt the most.

They'd been friends for years and years. Billy couldn't remember when they were *not* friends— going to school together, going to church together, belonging to the same Cub Scout troop. Their parents were friends. After church on Sunday they sometimes all went to the Radisson Hotel for the buffet brunch, and he and Shawn piled their plates sky high, made a game out of seeing who could eat the most. They rode their bikes together all over town, and sometimes their fathers took them fishing. Church camp in the summer. Boy Scout camp. And the band—Shawn had talked him into playing bass drum and they joined together. Shawn was more like a brother, closer than Richie.

The timer buzzed. Billy took the cake out of

the oven, put a platter on top of the skillet as described in the directions, and flipped the whole thing over. But when he lifted off the skillet, half the cake had dropped out onto the platter and the rest, the gooey stuff with all the pineapple, stuck to the pan.

Scraping at the sugary goo, Billy realized that in the past couple of days, he missed Shawn more than he missed Tanya. His throat began to ache when he thought about losing his friendship with Shawn.

But he could lose it, probably *would* lose it, if he didn't figure out a way to explain to Shawn what all this meant. Right now Shawn was mad because he'd nominated Billy for student council representative—three were to be elected from each class—and when Billy came out in support of the strange Jewish girl who was screwing up the band, it looked bad for Shawn.

Tonight at Teen Disciples, he'd talk to Shawn. He'd tell him about the threatening note Pazit had received. He'd try to explain how Pazit felt. It wasn't her fault; it was really that ACLU, that Anti-Christian Losers Union. He'd make Shawn see that this was something he, Billy, had to do—he was sorry, but that's how it was. And Shawn would understand.

Supper was pretty quiet. Billy was relieved. It seemed they had decided to let last night slide, pretend it didn't happen. Brenda unwound the bacon from her stuffed frank, but his parents seemed to like theirs. Then Billy brought his upside-down cake to the table.

"Looks more like an inside-out cake," his father said, eyeing the dessert.

His mother and sister were on their perpetual diets and wouldn't touch it, and Billy had forgotten that his father didn't like pineapple. Now that a big chunk of it sat in front of him, Billy wasn't hungry anymore.

BILLY WAITED BY the door of the fellowship hall for Shawn to arrive. He wore Pazit's Star of David shirt under a green-and-black striped rugby shirt. He was too warm, as he knew he'd be, but he wanted to get used to knowing the shirt was there. And maybe, if his talk with Shawn was a good one, he'd take off the top shirt, like Clark Kent turning into a Jewish Superman.

"Hey," Billy said when Shawn came in from the parking lot. "I got to talk to you."

Shawn gazed at him coolly. "What about?"

"About the band. About what's happened."

"I don't think there's much to talk about."

"Look, I'm real sorry," Billy said. "I didn't mean to be a traitor. That wasn't the idea. I guess I just didn't think about the outcome."

"I guess you didn't."

Brother Kent Secrist, the youth pastor, stuck his head around the corner. "Let's go, fellows."

"OK," they both said, but neither of them moved.

"Love thine enemy," Billy reminded Shawn. "Forgive those who trespass against you. I said I'm sorry."

Shawn shrugged. "OK. You're sorry. So you opened your mouth and put both feet in it. We all make mistakes, right? The question is what are you going to do about it?"

"Do?"

"I think you ought to make an apology to the band. Stand up and admit you made a mistake. People are really pissed, you know."

"But I didn't make a mistake. I did what I thought was right."

Shawn's ruddy face got redder. "I thought you said you were sorry!"

Billy clenched and unclenched his fists at his sides. "I'm sorry everybody's upset. I'm sorry everything is screwed up. But I guess I'm not sorry I said what I did, because I still think I was right."

"Look, with that attitude, you can kiss student

council good-bye. You can kiss Tanya Evans good-bye, too, and that I know for a fact."

This wasn't going at all the way Billy had planned it. He didn't want to discuss Tanya. He didn't want to discuss student council. What he wanted to talk about was Pazit and the note she'd found in her locker and what they could do to help her—even if she'd made him promise not to tell. But helping Pazit was the last thing he'd bring up to Shawn now.

"Shawn? Billy?" It was Brother Kent again.

Billy looked for a place where there were two seats together, but Shawn deliberately went to the opposite side of the room.

"Let us pray," said Brother Kent. Billy bowed his head, but his mind raced all over the place, like his hamster the time it got loose. He couldn't concentrate on the prayer, until Brother Kent said, "In Jesus' name we pray," and Billy mumbled, "Amen."

He sat down. The pastor started plunking on his guitar. "Jesus, Lord above all lords, Blessed Redeemer," Brother Kent sang in a sweet tenor voice.

Do it now, said a voice inside Billy's head, *All he had to do was yank off his rugby shirt, and the rest would take care of itself.* He pictured Pazit's hurt and angry face, her thick eyebrows knit together, when she showed him the note. *Do it, Billy. Do it.* But Billy ignored the voice.

Hard Hearts

THE PRESENCE OF Pazit's T-shirt in his bottom drawer lay as heavily on Billy's conscience as a broken commandment. After he'd lost his nerve and kept it covered up at Teen Disciples on Wednesday, he hadn't put on the shirt again. And now it was hard to face Pazit.

At school on Friday Billy had felt the anger growing and spreading like goose grass in a manicured lawn. And not only among the band members—everybody else seemed to be infected, too. A few kids tried to bring up the subject in class, but the teachers sidestepped the issue.

"This isn't the place to discuss it," Ms. Salton, the language arts teacher, had said. "It's a legal issue, and it has to be settled by legal means, no matter what the rest of us may think."

Billy had raised his hand. "This is like history being made right here at Jericho, and I think we ought to be able to talk about it. At least say what we *think*. I feel like we're being muzzled or something."

"I'm just telling you what I've been told, Bill." She always called him Bill, almost the only person who did, and he liked her for that. "A memo on the subject came around from the principal's office, advising us not to speak to the press and to refrain from classroom discussion as long as this matter is in litigation. 'Litigation' means what, class?"

"Arguing," announced one of the girls who always knew the meaning of everything, "about legal stuff."

Billy slumped down in his seat. Ms. Salton was one teacher he could usually get involved in real-life discussions, one who didn't just stick to the book. But this time, when it really mattered, he couldn't budge her.

Also on Friday he'd tried one more time to talk to Shawn, to make plans to get together, but Shawn told Billy that he and his family were going away for the long weekend to visit his grandparents in Hot Springs. Billy wished his family were going someplace. His mother had the whole three days off, but his dad had to keep the store open. Labor Day was always a big time for the home-improvement business, the day everybody decided to do the stuff they'd let slide all summer. The holiday weekend stretched ahead of him, empty and lonesome as a country road.

SATURDAY MORNING Billy rode his bike downtown to mow the grass, first at the Shoemakers', then at the Trujillos'. They'd had more rain on Thursday and bright sunshine on Friday, so the grass and weeds were thriving.

The big reason he wanted to go down to the Trujillos' was to talk to Pazit. He figured that after he'd finished with the yard, they'd sit out on the patio and talk, like the last time. There was something important he wanted to ask her: *What's it like to be Jewish?* If he was going to wear her Star of David shirt, he needed to know more about that. And maybe he'd explain to her why he hadn't worn it yet, and why it was so hard for him to put it on, mostly because he wasn't sure how his family would react. He figured the other kids would give him trouble, but it was his mom and dad that really worried him.

Then it turned out Pazit wasn't even at home. He was too shy to ask where she was when Mrs.

Trujillo came out to greet him, but later he noticed that the dog wasn't in his pen.

"Where's Tripper?" he asked when the boys came out to watch.

"Pazit taked him to the doctor," the smaller boy said. "For his itches."

"To the vet?"

"Yuh."

"So do you know when they're coming back?"

"Huh-uh. Maybe pretty soon."

Billy shooed the boys into the house for safety's sake. By the time he'd finished, the ragged weeds cropped close and the edges squared up so that it resembled a real lawn, Pazit and Tripper still weren't there. He didn't want to spend much time fooling around, afraid it would look like he was trying to pad out the time so he'd make more money. Even with the edging it took him little more than an hour, but Mrs. Trujillo insisted on paying him ten dollars. "I'm sorry Pazit's not here," she said, handing him two fives. "I know she'd love to talk to you."

Love to? Billy doubted that.

"But I'm glad I've got a chance to tell you again what a brave thing you did the other night," she continued. "It couldn't have been easy, getting up in front of all those people and saying what you did."

Billy looked down at his feet. "Yes, ma'am."

"I know I was scared spitless when I got up there and tried to say my piece. It's really tough speaking out when you're in a minority, but I think that's what we have to do. I hope people haven't been giving you a bad time about it."

"Not really," he lied.

"Well, I'm proud of you, and I'm sure your parents are, too, even if they don't agree with you. Pazit is thrilled to have a friend like you."

Thrilled. Oh man. Parents really don't know what they're talking about most of the time, Billy thought, *at least when it comes to figuring out what their kids think.* "Tell her I'll call her later," he said and backed carefully away.

THE HARPER HOUSEHOLD was in an uproar when Billy got home. His mother was on the phone in the kitchen, inviting other Band Booster parents to come over for "a strategy session," he heard her say. Tanya and Ashleigh Reynolds and some other girls from the drill team crouched over a huge banner spread out on the family-room floor. They were painting red letters on the white background:

THE DEMONETTES SAY:
WE *Love* OUR BAND!

"Love" was written in black script across a big red heart.

Tanya went through a big show of ignoring Billy, letting him know exactly how much she wasn't speaking to him, all the while yakking a mile a minute to Brenda. As far as Tanya Evans was concerned, Billy Harper had ceased to exist.

OK, he decided, he'd ignore her back.

But what was he going to do that evening? Every Saturday night for a year, with hardly any exceptions, he and Tanya had done something together—watched videos with Twig and Ashleigh or gone to some event at school or at church. Now Shawn was in Hot Springs, Brenda would be going out with Chuck, and Twig and Ashleigh would be wrestling in some dark corner with the TV turned up loud to muffle Ashleigh's squeals. He wondered what Tanya had planned but promised himself not to ask her, no matter what.

He thought about calling Pazit. Maybe they could just talk on the phone for a while. But somehow he didn't get around to it, since his mother had the phone tied up most of the afternoon. When Mr. Harper came home from work, Mrs. Harper sent him out again with a list of things to pick up at the supermarket. He came back with a large cake with Good Luck Pride of Demon Country scrolled in red script on the white icing. He had also brought barbecued ribs, potato salad, and slaw for the family's dinner.

Billy's parents had little to say to him as they hurried through their meal. Then his mother mentioned that she hoped he'd come to the party.

"It would be a good chance," she said, reaching for some coleslaw, "for you to explain why you said what you said the other night. People don't understand that you were just trying to be a good Christian because you felt sorry for that girl, and not because you're opposed to the cross or playing the hymns or anything like that."

"*You* explain, Mom," Billy pleaded, chewing on a rib. "I don't want to have to explain anything."

"I think you have to get it through your thick skull, Billy," his father said, "that you've put this family in a very embarrassing position."

Billy kept his eyes on his plate. He had been hanging his head about this for what felt like forever, and he was sick of it. He was sick of apologizing, and he wasn't even sure he had accomplished anything. No one seemed to have even heard what he said, except Mrs. Trujillo, who thought he was a hero of some kind. Big deal.

When the first of the guests began to arrive at seven-thirty, Billy went to his room and closed the door. He tried to concentrate on one of his dad's outdoors magazines. The minutes crept by. After a while there was a knock on his door and his mother peeked in.

"Billy, honey? Would you come down here for a second? We just need to ask you something."

Billy eyed his mother carefully and swung his feet off the bed. "About what?"

"We're organizing a rally in support of the band, for Wednesday afternoon. What we want is for the kids to get together and have a rally around the flagpole right after school, to sort of kick it off. Brenda's going to get the Demonettes there, and I just thought it would be nice if you'd get some of your pals . . ." She trailed off.

"But I'm *in* the band," he argued. "If the rally is supposed to support the band, that makes me look like I'm supporting myself. I mean, doesn't it?"

"If that's how you want to look at it, that's your privilege," she said, her face sagging. "But I just thought, since all of this has happened, maybe it would be a good thing for you to show your support of Mr. Dalrymple and the other kids in

215

the band, who maybe think you're on the wrong side."

He hated this. She looked so hurt, and like it was *his* fault that she was hurt, so he'd feel guilty. Mrs. Trujillo thought he was a hero, and his own mother thought he was a traitor. Billy didn't think he was either one.

She gazed at him from the doorway. "I see you've hardened your heart," she said sadly and went away.

Hardened your heart. Billy lay back down and tried to remember who it was he'd read about who had hardened his heart.

The answer came to him the next morning in church: it was the Pharaoh. God sent one plague after another on the Egyptians to make the Pharaoh let Moses lead the Israelites out of Egypt. First the Pharaoh would give in, but then after God relented and ended the plague, the Pharaoh would change his mind. During the sermon Billy flipped through the pages of the Old Testament until he found the passage in Exodus: "And Pharaoh hardened his heart at this time also, neither would he let the people go."

Pazit's people, Billy thought suddenly. *That's who Moses was leading out of Egypt. That's who the Pharaoh hardened his heart against: the Jews.* Billy

216

slapped shut the Bible so noisily that people around him turned to look.

THERE WAS NO way to skip Sunday brunch. They went to the Radisson like always, even though the Stovalls were away. Lots of people from Jericho Bible Temple were there, though, as well as other churchgoers: Mr. and Mrs. Evans and Tanya. It was embarrassing to keep running into Tanya at the buffet table. Tanya kept up her pretense of not knowing Billy was even on this planet while gushing all over Brenda and being super-polite to Mr. and Mrs. Harper. A neat trick, Billy thought sullenly, wishing he really *was* on another planet.

With Pazit.

Letters to the Editor

"INCREDIBLE!" Gus Trujillo exclaimed. "Absolutely beyond belief!"

He had spread out the Sunday morning *Jericho Advocate* on the patio table. Ellen had taken the little guys to her church. Gus refused to go to church, saying he had a great deal of respect for whatever people want to believe, but he personally didn't want to be involved. That left Pazit and Gus alone for some "one-on-one," as Ellen called it.

This was Pazit's favorite time of the whole week. Her and her father's idea of "one-on-one" was to sit with their coffee mugs and look over the paper together. Mostly Pazit flipped through the comics while her father worked his way through every section of the paper except sports. She had barely finished "Outland" when Gus got to the editorial page. "This is incredible. Look at this, Pazit."

She hung over his shoulder and read:

The student who disagrees with what music is being played should move on to another place. Don't make everyone suffer because of a few outsiders who want to turn this into a godless communist country.

"That's me," she said, sitting down again. "The outsider."

"But did you see who signed the letter?" He pushed the paper in front of her. "Albert Shoemaker. Our next-door neighbor."

The arrival of the daily paper was now a major event in Pazit's house. Since the story had broken on Wednesday, the newspaper had run at least one front-page news article about the high-school band every day, and the coverage kept getting bigger. The paper had even created a special logo, a drawing of a boy in a band uniform playing a bass drum labeled "Jericho," which they ran at the top of the main band story each day.

"You know, this could turn really ugly," Gus said.

"Ummm." Of course it could! It already had! Pazit wished her father had thought of what might happen before he'd called the ACLU. She thought of the note on lined yellow paper, still in the bottom of her book bag, the whispers of *"Jew bitch,"* and the mean looks shot at her like poisoned darts, but so far she had not told her father about any of it. There was nothing he could do that would make anything better.

"I don't like the tone of these letters at all," Gus said. "Here's someone writing about how his ancestors came to this country to escape religious persecution, but it doesn't seem to occur to him that that's exactly what he's doing now—persecuting somebody because of her beliefs. Human beings," he said, shaking his head sadly, "are really very strange people."

"You want some more coffee?" Pazit asked.

"Thanks," her father said absently. His nose was buried in the paper again. "And I wouldn't mind another cheese danish."

Every Sunday Gus brought danish pastries from the bakery as a special treat for Pazit; she didn't have the heart to tell him that these pastries bore little resemblance to the ones Ruth bought in Denver. Pazit's contribution to their Sunday luxury was *café con leche,* coffee with boiled milk.

By the time she carried the *café* and danish out to the patio, her father had found another infuriating letter. This one labeled the American Civil Liberties Union as the "Anti-Christian Liberals Union."

Then when Ellen came home with Brian and Matt, they went through the whole thing again, Gus reading the letters aloud, saving the one from Albert Shoemaker for last.

"Do you think they know who it is?" Ellen asked, draining the last of the coffee.

"Probably not," Gus said.

"Billy says they're a couple of old grouches," Pazit said. "They don't pay him what he should get, but he has to do it because they go to his church."

"Speaking of church, not one word was said about this at Holy Trinity this morning," Ellen complained. "Not one word! Can you believe it?"

"Did you expect some outcry?" Gus asked mildly.

"Yes! I certainly did! I assumed the people at my church would have a more liberal view, and they'd speak up. But when I buttonholed Father Pat after the service, he said he felt there was divided opinion in the parish and it was better not to bring it up than to make an issue of it and polarize the group."

Gus looked at her fondly. "I'm sure you set him straight."

"Well, I *tried*. But he really didn't want to hear it, at least not at coffee hour." She kicked off her shoes and stretched out on the chaise. "Hey, you guys," she said. "I think it would do us all good to get out of town. How about if we throw together a picnic and drive up to Fulton Dam. That's a patriotic, all-American thing to do on Labor Day weekend, right?"

"Suits me," Gus said.

"Yay! Picnic, picnic!" the little guys cheered.

"Can we take Tripper?" Pazit asked. "I bet he'd like to go swimming." That wasn't the real reason she wanted to take Tripper. She was afraid to leave the dog home alone, in case whoever wrote that note decided to do . . . something.

"Sure, why not? And if there's anybody else you want to invite, Pazit, that would be just fine."

She shook her head.

"Like your friend Billy Harper. How about him?"

"No," she said.

"Just like that? *No?*"

She remembered his promise on Wednesday to wear the shirt, and as far as she knew, he still hadn't done it. The whole school was turning against her, and he'd said he'd wear it, but he

222

didn't keep his promise. "He's not so great," she said.

"Is something wrong?" Ellen asked in that earnest tone that annoyed Pazit to death. "I thought he acted a little funny when he came to mow the grass yesterday. But I assumed that was because you weren't here and he expected you to be and he was too shy to say anything."

"Billy was here? Yesterday? Where was I?"

"It was while you were at the vet with Tripper. I forgot to tell you. He came right after you left, and he was gone by the time you got back. I thought he was kind of hanging around waiting for you, but I could have been wrong."

She shrugged. "I don't know if he was or if he wasn't. But I don't want to invite him on any picnic."

"OK, OK," Ellen said, throwing up her hands. "It was merely a suggestion."

They made tuna and egg sandwiches and packed a carton of strawberries and half a bag of gingersnaps that had gone soft in the humidity and a bottle of cranberry cocktail. Matt and Brian put in a few dog biscuits for Tripper. Ellen dashed back into the house to get an old blanket.

Pazit climbed in the broad backseat of Ellen's station wagon, called "Hog" because it burned so much gas. She sat in the middle with Matt belted on one side of her, Brian on the other, and Tripper and the picnic basket behind her. Gus drove, heading north to the dam.

The air conditioner had given up, as usual, and they rode with the car windows down. Hot, humid air whipped Pazit's hair. She gazed out at the flat landscape rolling past them. That was another thing that was wrong with this place—no mountains. Suddenly she was caught by an unexpected wave of homesickness for the Rockies, for Denver, for her other life.

Her life now was definitely worse than it ever had been before. Even in the bad old days, when Pazit was locked in daily combat with her mother, she'd had plenty of friends to rely on, especially Rachel.

She'd never felt this much of an outsider, even in Israel. She and Rachel had arrived at the school outside of Tel Aviv, exhausted after the long trip, but excited and a little scared of what it was going to be like—a different country, a different culture, a different language.

But she'd had hardly any chance to feel strange or out of place. The very next day she and Rachel had been cruising comfortably up and down the halls of the dorm where they'd been assigned to live with sixty other girls, some of them American, some from European countries, a few from Russia, but all of them Jewish. Pazit knew then that everything was going to be all right.

Pazit had many heated discussions with one of her roommates, Lindsay, a beautiful girl from Phoenix, Arizona, who had wealthy parents and tons of clothes. Her parents had sent her to school in Israel to get her away from her boyfriend, a guy named Ricardo whom her parents disapproved of because he was Mexican American. "They're absolutely petrified that I'll marry him, or have a baby with him," Lindsay confided. "I think that would be neat, though, having Ricardo's baby."

"What are you *talking* about, having a baby?" Pazit demanded. "Have you lost your mind? What would you do with a baby?"

"Love it," Lindsay declared, gazing at a photograph of a guy with a lot of dark hair and white teeth. "The trouble with you, Pazit, is you've never been in love," Lindsay accused her. "Or you'd know how I feel about him."

"This is true. I don't intend to fall in love for quite some time, and I certainly don't need to think about getting married and having babies. I might not even *get* married," Pazit had added.

"Everybody wants to be in love," Lindsay said.

"Not me. All I want is to have friends and to have a good time. I don't need a boyfriend."

That was before Pazit had met Leon. A few

months later Lindsay was throwing Pazit's words back in her face: "'I don't intend to fall in love for quite some time. I don't need a boyfriend.' See, Pazit, I told you you'd change your mind!"

Pazit had taken the friends, the good times, and later, the boyfriend all for granted. By the time she left she had at least a dozen friends who had promised to write to her. Some actually had. Lindsay sent a letter saying she had broken up with Ricardo and fallen in love with an Israeli soldier. "Long-distance love is too hard," Lindsay wrote. "But now my parents are having a fit about Sharón. They can't decide whether to leave me here or to bring me back to Phoenix."

Pazit knew what Lindsay meant about long-distance love: it was now exactly a hundred days since she'd seen Leon and he seemed farther away than ever. And things in Jericho had definitely *not* worked out the way she'd assumed they would. Except for Billy Harper, she did not have one friend.

When the family reached the dam they discovered that hordes of other people had had the same idea. First they drove around looking for a parking place, and then they walked around looking for an empty picnic table as the little guys got crankier and crankier. Finally they spread the old blanket on the rough, rocky ground and gobbled their lunch.

Gus wanted to read, but the little guys tried to coax him into going fishing and were not swayed by the fact that they had no fishing gear. Finally Pazit suggested taking Tripper on his leash down to the bank of the lake. There she showed the boys how to make boats out of leaves with tiny wildflowers for passengers. They sailed them in the murky water and seemed to be having a great time until Matt got stung by a yellowjacket.

"Your usual miserable sort of picnic," Ellen said as they headed home with the whimpering Matt cradled in her lap. "Tomorrow's Labor Day. What can we possibly do for an encore?"

"Stay home," Pazit muttered.

"I'm with you, Pazit," Gus said.

"I want to go fishing!" Brian pestered. "You promised, Daddy!"

"I'll teach you a game," Pazit told her brother. "It's called Fish. You'll like it. You'll probably win."

"Yeah!" Brian said, satisfied.

Having another day of freedom before she had to go back to school was a relief. The best thing about the week ahead was that it was only four days long. But it was going to be a tough week: since Mr. Dalrymple had announced they wouldn't use the cross formation, Pazit had made up her mind to march with the band after all. She liked to march. It was fun—or it used to be. And it counted for P.E. credit. She liked playing the music and didn't really mind that they were hymns as long as she didn't think about the words of the songs. But Pazit didn't really know if she could handle having ninety-four people against her. Next Friday night was the first football game of the season, and she knew that nobody, not even Billy Harper, would forgive her if they messed up because of her.

She would have to show them that she was a good musician, and if they gave her half a chance, she could march as precisely as any of them. She'd show them that even if they disliked her, they couldn't drive her away. They could win the championship, and she would help them. It was a matter of pride for her. But it was also very scary.

WHEN THE FAMILY got home from the picnic, there was a message on the answering machine for Pazit from Ruth. Guiltily Pazit realized that she had completely forgotten about her mother's Sunday call.

"Aren't you going to call her back?" Ellen asked.

"Later," Pazit said. But she didn't want to have to answer her mother's questions about school. She hadn't even told her mother about the band—it was too complicated. The main problem, though, was that Ruth would want to know if Pazit was coming home for the holidays. And every time she tried to make up her mind about whether to go or not, Pazit felt as though she was being torn into little pieces.

PART FOUR

Opening Game

Another Bellyache

"BAND!"

"Sir!"

Pazit snapped to attention.

"I'm sure it's clear to all of you that we still have a long way to go to be ready for Friday night's game," Mr. Dalrymple barked. "That's two days from now! Concentration, people—that's the key! You know your music, although the revision of 'A Mighty Fortress,' which we're now calling 'Tribute to Landis,' is still ragged. And you have all of the marching routine in good shape, except for the new ending, which seems to be very slow coming together. It's not your fault, and I know this hasn't been easy for you. When we get it right, I think it will knock their socks off. As of right now, though, we're in trouble. Do your best and we shall overcome!"

Pazit had taken her place on the field with the band for the second day in a row. It wasn't hard to sense their loathing in the way they held themselves stiffly apart from her. Two of the flutes had yielded her a position in the line, but they let her know with their cold stares that she didn't belong there.

Pazit had to scramble to keep up with the intricate marching pattern. It was much harder than she'd expected to take those precise twenty-two-and-a-half-inch steps, frontward *and* backward, sometimes sliding sideways with her feet moving one direction and her body facing another; maintaining the proper distance, elbows held just so; and always playing, playing, playing, without missing a note. Playing on the sidelines for two weeks hadn't given her the practice she needed. And of course, as Mr. Dalrymple had reminded her several times, she hadn't been to band camp. Twice she stumbled over her own feet, and several times she turned the wrong direction and crashed into someone. "Sorry," she muttered, "sorry, sorry, sorry."

Pazit expected Mr. Dalrymple to bawl her out when she screwed up—he was always yelling at somebody—but he didn't say a word to her. In a way that made it worse. She guessed he was simply going to let her make a fool of herself and die of humiliation.

After the band had been dismissed, Pazit took her time putting her flute away so she wouldn't have to walk back to the school with the rest of the band. Kneeling on the scuffed ground, she saw the feet. Several pairs, mostly in sneakers, were joined by more feet. The feet surrounded her. She looked up into a dozen pairs of eyes, all glaring down at her, and rose slowly.

"What?" she asked.

"Bitch," someone said, but Pazit couldn't tell who it was.

"Nobody's making you stay in the band," said Darla Jean, the flutist who marched next to her. "You'd make everybody a lot happier if you got out."

"Listen, why don't you just quit?" said another, shriller voice. "I mean, get out of the band, get out of the school, get out of *town!*" It was a trumpeter, a girl with pale blue eyes—Michelle Something.

"You're a real whiner, you know that? Got to have everything your way!" sneered a short boy who played the glockenspiel. "Well, this is a free country, in case you hadn't figured that out by now," he said, pressing in close, "and you can't go around making people do whatever you want, like they do in whatever commie country you came from."

"Just because you're a Jew you think you can come here and take over," said the red-haired bari sax player. "Well, nobody wants you here!" Their voices got louder as their confidence grew.

"Just get out, that's all." It was a good-looking boy from her theater class who was the teacher's favorite and kind of a star. He spit on the ground, near her feet.

Pazit stared back at them, shaking uncontrollably, feeling the adrenalin rush but determined not to let them see that they had succeeded in hurting her and scaring her. She was angry as well—furious, in fact. It was all she could do to keep from telling them what she thought they could do to themselves, using one of her father's more colorful phrases. But she bit her lip and kept quiet. *It was one of these,* she thought, *who wrote the note.*

"Jew bitch," snarled one of the girls. Then the group marched off, sticking tight and looking smugly self-satisfied.

Pazit picked up her flute and wiped her nose on her sleeve. Wasn't there one single person on her side? Where, for instance, was Billy? She thought she'd seen him, walking by himself as though he was in a daze. First he'd come around and made a big deal out of borrowing her Mogen David shirt. But he still hadn't worn it, at least not that she'd seen. So what *was* his point?

PAZIT MOVED THROUGH her morning classes like a robot, scarcely aware of what was happening. Instead, her head churned with the confrontation on the field: *"Jew bitch"* . . . *"Get out"* . . . *"Nobody wants you"* . . . *"Get out, get out!"*

She skipped lunch and stopped by the nurse's office to see Mrs. Wells. It had been a week since she'd been here and talked to the kind-eyed woman. Her stomach told her it was time.

Mrs. Wells looked up from a stack of paperwork with her soft smile and then frowned. "My my," she said. "You look exactly like somebody who has been drug through a knothole. Backwards," she added. She cleared a batch of file folders off the chair next to her desk. "I read in the papers about the battle going on. 'The Battle of the Band,' they're calling it. Sounds like you got cause for a first-class bellyache this week."

Pazit nodded, sat down, and tried to smile. Instead she burst into tears. "I hardly ever cry," she protested between sobs. "Not in front of people."

Mrs. Wells handed her a tissue. "Better if you do. That's why the good Lord gave you tears, for goodness sake."

Pazit honked into the tissue. "I can't believe how horrible they are," she said in a thick voice.

"People get mean when they're afraid they might be wrong. Or afraid they're gonna lose something. So they end up blaming you for what's their own fault."

"They're all blaming me, that's for sure."

"All of 'em? You haven't got one single soul on your side in all of this? One skinny little girl against everybody?"

She didn't like being called a skinny little girl, but Mrs. Wells was being so nice that Pazit forgave her. "Maybe one. I'm not sure. He's a drummer in the band. His name is Billy."

"Tall kid? Kind of curly hair? Glasses?" She demonstrated her description with her hands.

Pazit nodded. "That's him."

Mrs. Wells nodded with satisfaction. "I know Billy Harper. Tell you something—having a boy like that on your side is worth a whole lot. Now," she said, "you fixin' to go back to class this afternoon? Or you want me to write you an excuse and send you home?"

"I'm OK," she said, although she knew she wasn't. "I'll go in a minute."

"Supposing we get you a little something to put in your stomach first." Mrs. Wells took a brown bag out of a miniature refrigerator in the corner. "Enough in here for both of us." She unwrapped a thick sandwich and offered half to Pazit. "Egg salad," she said. "Homemade bread. Baked it myself."

Suddenly Pazit was ravenously hungry. "But that doesn't leave much for you," she apologized.

"Leaves enough."

They ate in a companionable silence, even sharing an orange and a cup of lemon yogurt. "My girl Yolanda used to be in the band," Mrs. Wells said as Pazit got ready to leave, "and I was real proud of her. I think she had some troubles a time or two, being black. She's on her own now, married and a mama. But I got to thinking after you were in here last week, and I decided it just isn't right for any band to be marching around with the *cross* to entertain folks at halftime. If Yolanda was still in that band, you bet I'd tell her she had no business using the most sacred symbol of her faith in such a lowdown way. If Yolanda was still there, honey, you'd have a friend, because she wouldn't march in any cross either."

Pazit smiled, but her lips were quivering. She was afraid she'd start to cry again. "Thanks for the lunch," she said in a husky voice.

Wrapped tight in her own misery, Pazit grabbed

her book bag from her locker after the dismissal bell and rushed out the side door. She noticed the crowd gathering around the flagpole in front of the school and remembered hearing an announcement over the P.A., something about a rally for the band. Obviously, that didn't include her.

Interview

A GIANT CARTOON of a red devil with a pitch-fork impaling a football lettered "Blainville," the team they would be playing Friday night, leaned against the main entrance to Jericho High School. Billy stood beside it and watched the crowd collect around the flagpole.

Mr. McBrayer, wearing a red satin Demon Country Booster jacket in spite of the heat, trotted up the broad steps, grinning like a game-show host. "Let's hear it for the Pride of Demon Country— the Jericho High School Marching Baaaaand!" he bawled, and the crowd cheered.

"Normally, I'd start this rally with a prayer, but under the circumstances, I guess I'd better not try *that* tactic!" Mr. McBrayer waited for the laughter that followed, plus some good-natured hisses and boos. "Now let's welcome the Demonettes!" he shouted, starting the applause.

The double doors swung open and the drill team, led by Brenda, pranced out in their short white skirts and red shirts and white boots. They waved their white cowboy hats above their heads in perfect unison, a gesture Billy had seen his sister practice with her friends for hours. They were followed by the Junior Demonettes, the colors reversed in their costumes, red skirts and white shirts. In the middle of the second group was Tanya, the prescribed drill-team smile pasted on her face.

In one practiced motion the girls put on their hats, all at exactly the same angle, and formed a triple line across the steps. Arms linked across each other's shoulders like a chorus line, they began wagging their heads back and forth, swaying and singing: "Love, love, love our band; We're going to win the fight," to the tune of "Row, row, row your boat." But the words got garbled when some of the adults tried to sing it as a round.

A lot of adults were out there, Billy observed, considering that it was the middle of the afternoon when most people were at work. He spotted his mother, who had taken a "personal day" from the bank to come. She had spent hours on the phone, organizing this rally. Incredibly, his father was with her, and Mr. Harper *never* took time off.

When the drill team finished their routine with hands-on-hips poses, lined up along the sides of the steps, Mr. McBrayer called on a few people to come up and address the crowd. Each one who did—mostly band parents, Billy saw, including his mother—complimented Mr. Dalrymple for his inspiring work and the band for their world-class playing and marching.

Mr. Dalrymple stepped forward to thank the Boosters for their loyalty and support. "Just remember," he said, "when the going gets tough, the tough get going. We'll do everything in our power to bring home another trophy from regionals in a little more than three weeks, and with God's help, we will! See you at the game Friday night!" That was the cue for the Demonettes to start the school song, "The Pride of Demon Country." Immediately the crowd joined in, singing so solemnly that Billy thought it sounded more like a hymn than a pep song.

Billy appreciated that everybody cared so much about the band and wanted them to win, but now it also bothered him. He had never thought before about the fact that *winning* the competition seemed more important than playing the music, more important than the people who played it.

His mind zigzagged to Pazit. He had seen her rush out the side door, probably fleeing for home. He didn't blame her. He wished he could have gone with her. Maybe he should have. So why didn't he? *Because,* said a voice inside his head, *you don't have the guts. She does what she believes is right. It's about time you did, too, Billy.*

From his place beside the demon, Billy watched a white van with the Channel 6 logo speed up the main driveway and halt behind the crowd. Immediately a camera crew emerged from the van. A sound technician handed a microphone to a good-looking man with a salon haircut and a flowered necktie, who was trailed by a TV camera. With an easy grin, the reporter sauntered toward a group of kids who had been listening to the rally speeches and watching the drill teams. Billy, curious, wandered over to join them.

From this new angle, Billy could see the huge banner that hung above the entrance to the school:

THE DEMONETTES SAY:
WE *Love* OUR BAND!

The crowd was still singing the school song, right index fingers raised signifying "We're Number

One." The camera operator panned that scene and then focused on the reporter.

"Hi," he said in a deep, mellow voice, "I'm Robin Robertson for Channel Six News. Anybody want to give me your reactions to what's happening here in Jericho?" Billy watched, hypnotized, as the kids crowded around the reporter, all anxious to talk.

"Yeah," said the popular football star, Jerry Winslow. Jerry stepped forward, his hands jammed in the pockets of his jeans. "This is a Christian community. Everybody here goes to church. So majority should rule, right? Only in Jericho it doesn't. Not when one person thinks she has a right to change everything."

A girl Billy didn't know flashed the reporter a huge smile. "Like, the band's been practicing since the first of August, they even went to band camp and learned all this stuff, and then *she* comes here from some other country, even, and doesn't know any of it, but it's like the people in the band don't count for anything."

The rally ended with more cheers and applause, and people began to drift away. Some saw the TV crew and stopped to watch. The crowd around the camera grew.

"We always win the regionals and place real high in the state competition," said Chuck Johnson.

"We're known as the Pride of Demon Country, and there's a whole caseful of the trophies we've won. You could take your camera in there and see it! But this year we might not win, because of this *one person*."

"Don't forget Mr. Dalrymple!" It was Twig Terwilliger, puffing asthmatically. "He started working out all this stuff last spring, and we all agreed, yeah, we wanted to do this religious theme, like we did a Western theme last year. And then this girl comes and screws up—pardon me—messes up the whole thing! And"—Twig paused dramatically—"we just wish she'd go back where she came from!"

Twig turned and stared directly at Billy. Billy stared back.

"Now tell me this," Robin Robertson said and paused for emphasis. "Is there anyone here who thinks maybe this *other* person might be right, or at least have a point?"

"No!" came the loud chorus.

The voice inside Billy's head spoke again. *Do it, Billy. You'll never have a better chance than this.*

Before he could think about the consequences, Billy called out, "Yes, I believe she's right." He had shucked his red-and-white Demons shirt, which the band was supposed to wear to pep rallies. Beneath it was Pazit's Star of David shirt.

The little crowd around the reporter moved aside, like the Red Sea parting for Moses, and Billy walked past them toward the TV camera that was pointed straight at him. "You agree with the dissenter?" the reporter asked, holding out the Channel 6 microphone to catch Billy's reply.

"Yes, sir," Billy said.

"And you're in the band?"

"Yes, sir. I play bass drum."

"And what's your opinion?"

"Everybody seems to think Pa—uh, I mean this girl—is trying to wreck things for the band and make them do it her way." His voice faltered but then grew stronger. "But that's not how I see it at all."

"Would you tell us how you *do* see it?"

"I guess if what we're doing hurts people who don't believe exactly like us, then it's up to us to stop doing it, that's all. I think we have to protect the rights of the minority, or we're a pretty lousy majority."

It was more than he had intended to say.

"I see you're wearing a Jewish star on your shirt," the reporter commented. "Any significance to that?"

"I'm just wearing the Star of David so she doesn't feel like she's alone."

"Thank you," the reporter said, stepping back

and turning to address the camera. "This is Robin Robertson for Channel Six, speaking to you from Jericho High School."

The crew hastily packed up their equipment. "Be sure to watch the six o'clock news!" the reporter called as he climbed into the white van and sped off.

Billy watched it go. Everyone else had gone, too, leaving him standing alone. Billy wished they'd let him explain. He was sure he could make them see, if they'd just *listen*. Billy walked slowly toward the bike rack.

He heard his mother calling, "Yoo-hoo, Billy!" and turned around to see them waving. He could tell by the smiles on his parents' faces that they hadn't heard the interview—and couldn't see the shirt he was wearing, either. "Want a ride home?" his mother hollered.

Billy shook his head. "Got my bike," he hollered back through cupped hands and watched his parents nod, wave, and head in the opposite direction, toward the visitors' parking lot.

Billy's was the only bike still chained to the rack. Even before he got there he could see that both tires were flat. And he didn't need to get any closer to know they had been slashed.

Happy Hour

GUS TRUJILLO FLIPPED on the evening news and settled in his usual spot on the couch in the TV room. Ellen arrived with her wine and Gus's beer and sat down on the floor with Matt. Brian snuggled under his father's left arm, and Pazit sat down on his right. She leaned close against him, holding a glass of orange juice. The little guys, who had a history of spilling, were only allowed cups of water during the family's daily Happy Hour.

"Well, how did it go today, *mi hijita?*" Gus asked, hitting the mute button during the commercial break. Vivid images of headache remedies and stomach soothers flashed by on the screen.

"It went," she said and decided to let it go at

that for now. She wanted to tell them about the kids who had surrounded her, but this wasn't the time. If there ever *was* a time! Even when she wanted to talk, there never seemed to be a good time for conversation. Everything was always in such chaos here, with Matt and Brian clamoring for attention, that it was hard to be heard.

Pazit was still not sure what she wanted her father to do about this trouble with the band. He was the one who had gotten her into it, he and the ACLU, but so far he hadn't done anything to get her out. If any of this had happened when her mother was around, everything would have been different.

Ruth Trujillo would have been over at the school the first time the cross was mentioned. She wouldn't have bothered to call up the ACLU, and she wouldn't have gone to the school-board meeting and made a quiet little speech.

Ruth Trujillo would have charged into Jericho High School and would have told Mr. Dalrymple in no uncertain terms what she thought of him telling a Jewish kid she was supposed to march in a cross formation. And then she would have burst into the principal's office, barging right past the secretary if she gave her any trouble or tried to delay her, and she would have ripped into the principal for letting it happen. If there had been any other teachers around, she would have blasted them as well.

Ruth Trujillo would have insisted that the kids who called Pazit names and told her to quit be hauled into the principal's office and punished. She would have taken the nasty note with threats about Tripper straight to the chief of police and demanded that the perpetrators be apprehended and brought to justice. She would have called the mayor of Jericho and the chairman of the school board. She would have found out where their offices were, and she would have gone there and made them listen.

She would have contacted the press, calling up the newspaper and the TV station, and she would have told them how her daughter's rights were being violated. And if that didn't get some instant action, Ruth Trujillo would have hired a lawyer, and she personally would have brought suit against the school and everybody connected with it.

It would have been quite a scene all around. Thinking about it made Pazit smile. You had to be proud of a mother who stuck up for you like that! But Pazit had not told her mother anything about her problems with the band. What could even a powerhouse like Ruth Trujillo accomplish all the way from Denver?

Pazit couldn't begin to imagine her father

rampaging through the school system. But then, she hadn't told him about the threatening note, or about the kids whispering *"Jew bitch,"* or about the kids who surrounded her this morning. He didn't know how bad it was. But even if he did, it wasn't Gus Trujillo's style to make a big stink—he was much too calm and rational for that—and she couldn't make up her mind if she was glad about that or not. Her mother's style could be horribly embarrassing.

"Oh, Pazit, I almost forgot," Ellen said as Tom Brokaw reappeared on the screen, "your mom called this afternoon."

"She did? Where was I?"

"Walking with Tripper. She wanted to know if you had made up your mind which days you were going to take off from school to go to Denver for the High Holy Days. She has to buy the ticket now to get a cheap rate."

"Go?" Gus said, catching the tail end of the conversation. "Go where?"

"To Denver," Pazit said. "For Rosh Hashanah."

"When is it?"

"Next week."

"I didn't know you were planning to go."

"I'm not *planning* anything. Mom wants me to."

"Can we talk about it later?" her father asked. "After the news?"

Pazit still didn't know what she wanted to do. She didn't care about missing school—that was no problem. Her dad could write her an excuse, and she'd figure a way to make up the work, which was stupid and boring anyway. And she was anxious to see her friends, and Denver itself. It wasn't just the fresh bagels she missed, it was the *whole* Jewish thing. The synagogue, the kosher cooking, the *Shabbat* candles. It was OK to be Jewish in Denver.

Pazit knew now that it wasn't at all OK to be Jewish in Jericho. If you weren't Christian, she'd learned, you were screwed. Pazit didn't consider herself an overwhelmingly religious person, although she did believe in God, she did think of herself as Jewish, and she did practice some Jewish rituals. That's just who she *was*. Maybe, when she got right down to it, that's what she missed most in Jericho: she had lost a part of who she was, no matter how hard Ellen tried not to mix up meat and milk. Her father probably would have taken her to a synagogue if there was such a thing around. But there wasn't. She hadn't even thought to ask before she came. She'd never been anyplace where there was no synagogue.

Pazit had not met one single Jew in Jericho. She had combed the local phone book looking for Jewish names and found a few that she was pretty sure were Jewish, but what was she supposed to do? Call up and say, "Hi, I'm Jewish, here I am in Jericho, what do I do now?"

While correspondents from the White House and the Pentagon and various U.S. cities talked earnestly on the TV screen, Pazit thought about going back to Denver for the holidays—at least for Rosh Hashanah, the beginning of the new year. If she went she couldn't miss school for the whole ten days, through Yom Kippur. She'd have to observe the Day of Atonement on her own. Last year, when she turned thirteen, was the first time that she had fasted for the entire twenty-four hours of Yom Kippur. Last year she had been in Israel for the holidays, and everybody on the kibbutz had been observing the fast. Not like here, where she'd be the only one.

But if Pazit went back to Denver even for a short visit, just for Rosh Hashanah, it would probably start things up all over again with her mother. Everything that was bottled up inside her would come spilling out, all the stuff about the band and the kids, all her anger at her mother for sending her here, even though Pazit had demanded to be sent. On the other hand, it would give her a chance to see Rachel, instead of settling for the frequent phone conversations.

She wanted to go. She didn't want to go.

Last Sunday when she'd finally called Ruth

back, Pazit had told her mother, "I don't know if I can, Mom."

"Look," her mother said, sounding exasperated, "you have until Wednesday to make up your mind. That's the last day I can get you an advance-purchase ticket, which is cheaper, and that's a consideration. Also, it's not particularly flattering that you can't make up your mind if you want to come see me or not. Is your life there so wonderful that you can't take four days to spend with your mother on this important holiday?"

"No," Pazit admitted. "It's not wonderful."

It's horrible, Pazit thought. *That's why I can't go there. Because I won't want to come back here.*

The national news ended, and the local news came on. Pazit went to get a refill on orange juice and heard both Dad and Ellen holler from the TV room. "Pazit! Come quick! Hurry!"

She rushed, slopping juice as she ran. "Look," her father said. "That's your school."

"This afternoon your Channel Six News crew visited Jericho High School," intoned the reporter, "where parents and students rallied in support of the band's right to include religious symbolism in its halftime performance." The screen showed the crowd gathered around the flagpole, then cut to a shot of a sign above the entrance to the building.

While the reporter was explaining the "Battle

255

of the Band," the station ran footage of last year's performance, showing the band in one of its intricate marching routines. Next they cut back to the reporter on the scene as he interviewed some of the students clustered around him. Pazit perched on the edge of the couch.

"This is a Christian community," some jock was saying. "So majority should rule, right?"

"My God," Gus breathed.

Next a thin girl with overdone eye makeup who Pazit recognized from her theater class complained about the girl who thought everything had to be done the way *she* wanted.

"I can't believe this," Ellen kept saying. "This whole thing is just so completely . . ."

"Hush!" Gus ordered.

And the cretin with the cymbals said, "We just wish she'd go back where she came from."

"Oh, Pazit," Ellen sighed, "you never said . . ."

Then, as the camera panned across the small crowd clustered around him, the reporter asked if anybody agreed with the other person's point of view. While the crowd yelled *No,* the camera cut to a tall boy with curly blond hair moving toward it.

"It's Billy!" Pazit exclaimed, moving closer to the TV screen to try to see him better.

She concentrated on every word as Billy made his case, so she could remember what he said. And at the end, when the camera pulled back and showed the shirt with the Mogen David, Pazit jumped up and down and clapped. "That's my shirt! Dad, Ellen, look—my shirt! He wanted to borrow it, and I let him have it, and now look!"

"I wish we had this on tape," Gus said. "This is just incredible."

"That kid has more courage than most of the adults in this town put together," Ellen said. "I will never forget how he stood up in front of all those people at the school board that night. And now look at him! I think you ought to call him, Pazit, and tell him how proud we all are of him."

They were all much too excited to watch the rest of the news or to wait for the weather report. Pazit, buffeted by a multitude of feelings—anger and resentment, gratitude, confusion, pride, pain—went to work fixing the salad for dinner. Ellen tossed a brick of frozen peas into a pan of water and took a roasted chicken and baked yams out of the oven. Gus cut up the chicken, Pazit poured milk for the little guys, more juice for herself, and got out margarine for the yams and peas so there wouldn't be any dairy served with the chicken. Everything involved in getting this ordinary meal on the table had an edge of excitement.

"We have a lot to talk about, Pazit," her father said, trimming the dark meat off a thigh bone.

"First of all, I'm deeply concerned about what's going on at that school. Have you been subjected to harassment?"

Pazit could hardly keep from laughing out loud. *Welcome to Planet Earth, Dad,* she thought. "Some," she allowed. "I guess you could call it that." She thought of the note she hadn't shown them, the confrontations she hadn't told them about. "Nothing I can't handle."

"I'm sure you can handle it—you're a very strong young woman. But whether you *can* is not the point," Ellen said. "It shouldn't be happening, period."

"I'm going to pay a visit to your principal, probably tomorrow," Gus announced. "I want you to come up to my study after supper and give me details, so I have it all in writing. All right?"

Pazit nodded. It wasn't the way her mother would deal with it, but it was something. She wouldn't tell him about the note, though. There were some things she just couldn't talk about.

"The next thing on the agenda," Gus said, "is this visit your mother wants you to make for Rosh Hashanah. Have you decided what you want to do, Pazit? It's entirely up to you, whether you go or not."

"I'm going," Pazit said, suddenly sure. "I'll call Mom right now and tell her."

Bad Luck

BILLY RAN TWO cans of barbecue beans through the electric can opener. He was dumping the beans in a saucepan when he heard a car in the driveway. He hoped it wasn't his parents. He was relieved to see Chuck Johnson's sleek red-and-white Mazda. Moments later Brenda stormed into the kitchen, her eyes puffy from crying.

"You!" she yelled. "I can't believe you, Billy!" She crumpled into her chair at the kitchen table. "Do you have any idea what you're doing, Billy? How bad this *hurts?*" Her chin was wobbling, and her eyes filled with genuine tears.

"How bad *what* hurts?" he asked, but of course he knew.

"You, wearing that awful shirt, telling the TV people you're sticking up for that Jewish girl, even though she's trying to wreck the band."

"She's not trying to wreck the band," Billy said wearily. "And I don't see how it hurts you if I wear a shirt with a Jewish star on it."

"Because it shows you don't have any loyalty. It shows you don't *care*—about your family *or* your school. We went through all this before, when you got up and opened your big mouth in front of the school board and we all thought you had lost your mind. But this is going to be on *television!* Are you in love with this Jewish girl or what?" She dug in her pocket for a tissue. "Because I'll tell you, if there's one thing Daddy won't stand for, it's any of us going out with somebody who isn't our religion. Remember when Richie dated that Italian girl in high school? And Daddy had a near fit because she was Catholic?"

"I don't remember," Billy said. He opened the refrigerator and pretended to search for the package of franks that was right in front of him. "But I don't see what that has to do with this. We're just friends, that's all. And even if I was going out with her, I'm fifteen years old and she's fourteen and I don't think we'd be planning on getting married anytime soon. So what difference does it make if she's Jewish?"

"You don't get it, do you, Billy? I mean, Jews have a very bad reputation. Everybody knows they try to take over everything, and all they're interested in is money. Just ask Daddy."

"That's stupid," Billy said, licking his dry lips. "I'll bet plenty of Christians are the same way." He slit open the package, dumped the franks in the pan with the beans, and turned the heat on low.

"No, they're not, Billy!" Brenda's voice rose shrilly. "People are different, and you don't want to believe it, because of this girl. Do you realize what you're doing to all of *us* just on account of *her?* How you're ruining the band's chances to win the competition? And everybody's morale has sunk about as low as it can get. Not just the band, but the Demonettes, too."

"The Demonettes aren't part of the band. This doesn't have anything to do with them. We just play the music for their routine." The more Billy tried to reason with her, the more he saw how useless it was.

"What makes you think it doesn't affect us? Maybe we're not in the same competitions, but we are in the same *school*. We all support each other. But I guess that doesn't mean much to you."

She was furious, but at least she wasn't crying anymore. Billy couldn't stand it when girls cried.

"It means a lot," he replied. "You don't believe me, but it does."

"And another thing," Brenda said, popping open a diet soda. "Look what you're doing to Tanya. You are breaking that girl's *heart*."

"How about what Tanya's doing to me?" Billy asked, although he knew Brenda wasn't interested in his side of the argument. "She won't even speak to me. She pretends I don't exist. I've tried to explain to her, like I'm trying to explain to you, but nobody listens!" Suddenly he smashed his fist on the table, and the saltshaker in the shape of a cactus clattered to the floor and broke. Brenda jumped.

"Wow," she said, staring at the mess. "What right *you've* got to be mad is beyond me. And I bet you won't be going around smashing things when Mom and Daddy get home. They are going to be real upset when they find out what you've been doing. They take time off from work so they can come to school and show their support for the band, and there's their *son* parading around in an ugly Jewish shirt and mouthing off against everything they stand for! How would you feel if it was your kid, practically thumbing his nose at your beliefs?"

"I'm not thumbing my nose at anything," Billy mumbled, picking up pieces of the broken cactus. "I'm only trying to stick up for somebody who everybody else is making out to be some kind of monster, just because she's a little bit different."

"A little bit! I'd say a whole lot!" Brenda sipped the diet soda and sounded calmer. "Look, you are my little brother. I feel like I ought to look out for you. By the way, it's bad luck, you know, spilling salt like that," she added, watching him sweep the salt into a dustpan and dump it in the trash.

"Just what I need, bad luck," Billy said through clenched teeth. He hated it when she talked down to him, but Brenda had always made a big deal out of being eighteen months older, teasing him because she'd always be ahead of him and he'd never catch up.

"Is that all you're making for supper?" Brenda asked, as he ripped open a package of buns. "Lately you've been doing this gourmet hot dog thing."

"Don't have time. I just got home. I had to walk."

"Walk? What happened to your bike?"

"Flat tires," he said. "Both of them. Somebody slashed them."

"Somebody slashed your tires? Hey!" Brenda perked up and looked interested. "Any idea who it was?"

"Somebody who doesn't like my opinions. Probably one of *your* friends."

"Here's my advice," Brenda said, ignoring his

remark. "Be smart and take off that damned shirt before Mom and Daddy get home."

"Does Dad know how you talk? You know he doesn't allow bad language."

"I don't do it in front of them," she said. "Anyway, I'm a senior and I'll be eighteen soon and I can talk any way I want to. And don't even think of telling Daddy, because he'll know you're just doing it to take the heat off yourself."

"I don't snitch," Billy said. Then he thought of something. "I don't suppose you'd know anything about the threatening note somebody sent Pazit, would you?"

Brenda's eyes widened. "A threatening note? What does it say?"

"It says if she keeps making trouble something bad will happen to her dog." Billy watched Brenda's face. "Probably something like what happened to my bike tires."

"My, my," Brenda said and drummed her fingers on the table.

"So you know who wrote it?"

"I guess you could say I have a pretty good idea who it might be."

"Who?"

Brenda snorted. "You are absolutely the last person in this world I would tell, Billy," she said and stalked out of the kitchen.

Billy examined the pieces of the saltshaker cactus, wondering if he could glue it back together. No time to worry about that now—his parents would be home any minute. He was surprised that they weren't already here; he'd expected them to come on home after the rally, but they had apparently gone back to their jobs.

Billy heard the garage door rumble open and his mother's car pull in. The door stayed up; she always left it up for his dad's pickup.

"I broke the cactus," Billy said when his mother came in. He showed her the pieces. "I'm sorry. Maybe I can fix it." He could tell from her clear, open face that she hadn't heard about the TV interview yet. And she didn't seem to have noticed the shirt.

Moments later his father arrived and went upstairs to shower and change clothes. Billy heard him come back downstairs and turn on the television in the family room to catch the local news and sports. From the kitchen Billy could see the big TV screen and the back of his father's head, his wet hair sticking up in dark spikes. His mother's curly blond head barely showed above the back of the sofa. Billy put the hot-dog buns under the broiler to toast.

Usually the Harpers watched Channel 11 because Billy's father liked the way they handled sports coverage, but not today. His father punched the remote and Channel 6 came up. "Did you see their news crew at the rally this afternoon, Brenny?" Dad said to Brenda, who had sidled in and sat down on an ottoman next to his recliner. "Let's see what they got."

Brenda turned and flashed Billy a taunting grin. Billy mentally tossed a coin: he could go to his room and wait for his father to come storming up the stairs, demanding an explanation, or he could stay here and watch, hoping the TV people had cut out his part, and then he'd be off the hook for a while at least. Until Brenda brought up the subject, which of course she would.

Billy made up his mind and leaned in the doorway, watching. In a way he was excited—he had never been on TV before, and under different circumstances this would have made him a celebrity at school.

It was all there, every word he said, plus a close-up of the shirt. "Oh my God," his mother moaned softly.

"Well, Billy," his father said sadly.

"In a minute," Billy said and hurried to yank open the broiler. The buns were charred. He dumped them in the garbage and put a loaf of white bread on the table. "Supper's ready," he announced, as though nothing had happened.

"We'll talk later," Mr. Harper said, his lips

tight. "I want to eat in peace. And I need time to think. Now let us go sit down and bless our food."

After they'd said grace, they ate in silence. Brenda looked over at Billy a few times with an I-told-you-so little smile. His father kept his eyes on his plate. No one said a word about the shirt.

"I'VE GOT TO talk to you," Billy told Shawn as soon as he had arrived at Teen Disciples.

"Go ahead," Shawn growled. "Talk. Then I've got something to tell *you*."

"It's too long to go into now," Billy whispered. "Brother Kent is going to be after us in a minute. Let's leave early. We could go out by the fishpond. Nobody'd bother us there."

Shawn shook his head. "Can't. I promised I'd get signatures on this petition." Shawn handed him a long white form.

WE THE UNDERSIGNED REQUEST THAT OUT OF CONSIDERATION FOR OTHER MEMBERS OF THE BAND AND THE HARD WORK THEY HAVE IN-VESTED, ANY BAND MEMBER WHO HAS NOT AT-TENDED BAND CAMP AND IS NOT WELL PREPARED SHOULD NOT BE ALLOWED TO PERFORM AT HALF-TIME OR AT ANY MARCHING COMPETITIONS.

Billy read it a second time, slowly. "This is to keep Pazit from marching," Billy said.

"Hey, you're right, Billy!" Shawn said in mock surprise. "No matter what you think of her and her religion, the girl screws up. She doesn't know the routine, and she's messing up the whole thing."

"Mr. Dalrymple can tell her she can't march, if he wants to," Billy said.

"Huh-uh. The Colonel has turned chicken. He's scared to death of lawsuits. He told Mr. McBrayer he won't do anything to cause any trouble. So it's up to us to get her out of there."

Billy read the petition again and scanned the list of signatures. There were already more than a dozen, including Shawn's and his parents. Then one name leaped out at him: *Cara Stovall,* her name printed in small neat letters, the *C* with a peculiar little loop that Billy recognized: the same *C* in "Christian" in the note sent to Pazit.

"I'm sorry," Billy said, handing back the petition, "but I can't sign it."

Shawn started to argue, but Brother Kent cut him short. "Fellows? Let's go, OK?"

Decisions

"Just don't get upset," Billy reminded Pazit quietly. "Don't let them see it's getting to you."

Following Billy's advice, Pazit tried to ignore the dirty looks as the band left the practice field and headed for their first period classes. It wasn't just Pazit they were glaring at, but at Billy, too.

Billy was wearing her shirt again this morning. The Mogen David sent her a reassuring message, although she still had not figured out why Billy was doing this. Pazit couldn't imagine putting herself out the way Billy was. It made her very curious: what could possibly be in it for *him?*

"There's a petition," Pazit said.

"I saw it. It doesn't mean anything."

"How can you say it doesn't mean anything?" Pazit demanded. "They'll get a lot of signatures and take it to Mr. Dalrymple, and he'll tell me to leave. So I'm thinking maybe I ought to just quit and save him the trouble."

The morning practice had not gone well. Mr. Dalrymple had yelled at them repeatedly for one botched move after another, and Pazit knew she was to blame for most of the mistakes. Everybody else knew it, too, and she could feel the rage all around her. Not all of the anger had been silent. Darla Jean, the flute next to her, had made it plain: "There's a petition against you," Darla Jean said. "Everybody signed it."

"Against me?"

"Because you're ruining everything for the rest of us. First you made us get rid of our cross and half of our music, and now you want to march, even if you don't know how and you make the rest of us screw up. We'll probably look like a bunch of fools tomorrow night at the opening game, and there's no way we can win the competition. All because of you!"

"Also," Pazit told Billy now, "I'm still worrying about Tripper. Maybe whoever sent me that note is still thinking about doing something to him."

"You don't have anything to worry about

there," Billy said. "I know who wrote that note, and I'm taking care of it. It's OK, honest."

"You found out? How?"

He tapped his forehead. "Call me Harper, P.I.," he said. "But I still don't know who slashed my tires. *That* I haven't figured out yet."

"You got your tires slashed? Was it because of me?"

"Not because of you. Because of what *I* said, I think. People around here get upset when you don't agree with them."

"I'm sorry, Billy," she said. What else was there to say? She reached out and touched his arm.

"I could help you," Billy offered. "I could meet you here after school this afternoon, and we could go through the routine together."

"Just the two of us?" she said doubtfully. "I don't see how that would work."

"Look—you know your music, you just don't know the moves. And I know the music and—believe it or not—I know not only my moves but most of the others, too. I've got a good memory for that stuff. I memorized it all from Mr. Dalrymple's computer printouts. So we go out on the field and I walk you through it a few times, and I'll bet you get it real quick. At least you could *try.*"

The building was in a state of controlled chaos

as students rushed to beat the late bell. "I'll think about it," she promised. Someone slammed into her and kept on going without apology.

For the first three periods Pazit tuned out the teachers—easily done—and tried to think what to do. She knew that her father wanted her to do whatever would make her happy, but he believed that what would make her happy was standing up for her rights. She knew, also, that her mother would not want her to back down. "This is the way it has been throughout history for us," her mother would say, as Pazit had heard her say about Jews in the past. "They'll try to make everything miserable for you just to get rid of you."

At lunchtime Pazit went to the cafeteria and bought a large red apple and a banana, two giant oatmeal cookies, and a can of orange juice. She dropped the food into her book bag and slipped into the nurse's office.

"Hi," Pazit said, checking to see if anyone else was there. Mrs. Wells put her finger to her lips and gently closed the door to the next room, where Pazit glimpsed a figure lying on the narrow cot under a cotton blanket.

"Got me a customer," Mrs. Wells explained. "You're just in time for lunch." Two halves of a thick sandwich lay on her desk.

"I planned it that way," Pazit said and produced the fruit and cookies from her bag.

"Hoooooh boy," Mrs. Wells said. "I'm cheating on my diet again." She laid part of her sandwich on a napkin and pushed it toward Pazit. "Your half."

Pazit peeked between the slices of brown bread. "Is that ham and cheese? I can't eat it," she said and pushed it back.

"Can't eat ham?"

"I'm Jewish and I keep kosher. Ham isn't kosher so I don't eat it. And cheese with any kind of meat isn't kosher either. So this sandwich is double-unkosher." She hesitated, not wanting to seem unappreciative. "But I bet I can fix it."

"Help yourself," Mrs. Wells said.

Pazit opened the sandwich halves, moved all the ham to one half and all the cheese to the other, and closed them up again. Technically not kosher, but in this case close enough, she decided. "Ham for you, cheese for me. OK?"

Mrs. Wells chuckled. "OK by me."

"You look better today," Mrs. Wells observed. "Maybe having that Harper boy stick up for you right on TV yesterday is making your stomach think the world isn't such a bad place after all."

"Maybe," Pazit agreed. "But I still don't know

what to do. The band's all mad at me because I keep messing up the marching. Somebody's passed around a petition to make Mr. Dalrymple throw me out. But Billy says he can teach me all the steps before tomorrow night's game and I'll be all right."

"And what can't you decide?"

"Because even if I learn the steps perfectly, which I doubt even Billy can teach me by tomorrow, they still don't want me there." She debated telling the nurse about the threatening note and then decided that since she had gone this far, she might as well go the rest of the way. "I got a note last week that said if I didn't stop trying to get them to give up their cross, they'd do something bad to my dog. They're still mad, because now they think they won't win the regional competition and they won't get to go on to state finals."

"And they say that's all your fault, right?"

"Right."

"Hmmm." Mrs. Wells took a bite out of the apple. "You're getting blamed for a lot that isn't any of your doing, that's my opinion. If they really wanted to win so bad, then more than your friend Billy would be trying to help you learn those steps. They'd *all* be knocking at your door, wanting you to come out and march this way and that with them, making sure you got it right. Now isn't this so? They could help you *and* they could win if they wanted to bad enough."

"I guess so."

"So it's my opinion that they're so busy being mad at you because you're not exactly like them, maybe you dress a little different or you talk a little different or you *believe* a little different, that they're forgetting all about what isn't so different, that you like to play music and you like to march. And unless I'm dead wrong, and I don't think I am, you're probably real good at it, too."

Pazit grinned. "I am. Or I used to be when I lived in Denver. We had a great marching band. As soon as the spring concert was over, Mr. Ramsey took us outside and we started learning to march. You know, exactly how long a step to take, how to keep the right distance between each player, all that. People said our middle-school band was better than lots of high-school bands."

Mrs. Wells held up a hand. "I believe you! No need to convince me!" She dabbed at her mouth with a napkin. "But it sounds like you're going to have to do more than *talk* to convince folks here. My thinking is, don't tell 'em, show 'em."

"I'm not sure *anything* would convince those kids."

The bell rang for fourth period. Pazit gathered up her trash and got ready to leave.

"Thank you for sharing your lunch," Mrs. Wells said. "But you better take that other cookie along with you. Give it to your friend Billy next time you see him."

IT WAS CREEPY, sitting through fourth period band. Mr. Dalrymple had them practice some of the pep songs they'd be playing from the stands, rehearsing the brass fanfares for when the Demons scored, running through the music to accompany the Demonettes for their routine. Everyone ignored Pazit. *I'll show you,* she thought to herself. *I really will show all of you.* But she wasn't so sure she could.

As soon as the last bell rang, Pazit hung around waiting for Billy to come by and show her the marching steps. But there was no sign of Billy. She hadn't seen him in fourth period band, which was odd. Poor Billy—he seemed kind of lost these past few days. *Not my problem,* Pazit thought, although part of her believed it really was. She struck out for home.

As she turned the last corner and started up Fourth Street, Pazit noticed a clunky old car pulling away from the curb. It might have been stopped in front of her house, but she was still too far away to know for sure. As she hurried up the front walk, braced for the usual quizzing by Ellen, Pazit saw the gaily wrapped package on the doormat. She picked up the package and read the tag attached to the red bow: *To Pazit.*

Pazit stuffed the package in her book bag and scooted down the hall past Ellen's studio, let the little guys assault her with sticky hugs, and then pried herself free and ran up to her room.

She nervously peeled off the white paper, slit the tape that sealed the box, and lifted off the lid. Inside was a nest of crumpled white tissue paper. In the center of the nest lay a dead rat, stiff and glassy-eyed. A little card was tucked in beside it: From Your Friends in the Band.

Pazit clapped the lid back on the box and sat down on her bed. She felt as though she had been punched. She tried to think what to do next: Hustle the corpse out to the trash and pretend it hadn't happened? Show Ellen and, later, Dad, knowing they'd go through the ceiling and call Mr. Dalrymple, the principal, the ACLU, the President of the United States? Tell Billy and hope he'd have some idea what to do?

Yes, she decided, *Billy.* She went to the phone in her father's study, looked up Billy's number, and dialed it, her fingers shaking. After four rings the answering machine clicked on, and a male voice, probably Mr. Harper's, instructed her to leave a message. She was tempted to hang up, but she didn't.

"Billy," she said in a quivery voice, "it's Pazit. Call me."

Evidence

"Go ahead. Open it."

Not knowing what to expect, Billy gingerly lifted the lid of the white box, which looked like something from a flower shop. He peered in and gasped. "Where did it come from?"

"I don't know," Pazit said, but she told him about the car she'd seen pulling away from the curb in front of her house.

"What kind of car?"

When she described the old maroon sedan, Billy recognized Twig's car. And the white box might have come from Ashleigh's Flowers. It really wasn't much of a mystery. He knew the people who had done this. Not just acquaintances either—his *friends.* But Billy wasn't ready to tell her that he knew who was responsible. Not yet. He had to think this through. "Have you told your folks?"

She shook her head. Her skin was usually pale, but now it looked ashen.

"Are you going to?"

"I don't know. I'm afraid all hell will break loose. And I just don't think I can stand any more." She paused and raked her fingers through her hair. "But you know who did it, don't you, Billy?"

Billy nodded unhappily. "I think so. I wish I didn't. But I guess we have to figure out what you want to do. I thought when you called you wanted to go practice marching. I told you I'd be glad to teach you. I meant it. But now . . . well, it's really up to you."

"How can I march with a group that sends me a dead rat? The note, the petition, the nasty whispers—I didn't let that get to me too much. But this is over the top. They *won,* Billy. It's that simple. They know I can't do it. Mrs. Wells says I should go out and show them, but how can I?"

"I know. I heard her."

"You heard Mrs. Wells say that?"

"I was on the cot in the next room. Stomach problems." He grimaced. "When I heard you out there, I listened."

"She didn't tell me it was you in there."

"She's OK, Mrs. Wells. I guess a lot of us have found out we can go talk to her about things we can't talk to anybody else about, and she keeps her mouth shut."

"Have you talked to her about the band?"

"Some."

The two of them were sitting in Pazit's back-yard. She had let Tripper out of his pen, and he lay contentedly at her feet, chewing on a rawhide bone. *At least,* Billy thought, *nobody had followed through on Cara's threat and done anything to the dog—yet.*

"You know what bothers me most," Billy said slowly—he had been going over and over this in his head for the past couple of days—"is that the kids who are doing this to you all go to church on Sunday. They grew up being taught to 'Love thy neighbor' and 'Do unto others.' And then when it comes right down to it, they act so hateful. Because they're not getting their own way, they get mad and blame everything on you because you're Jewish. This whole business just makes me sick!"

One of Pazit's little brothers ran out from the house and stopped a few feet away, staring at Billy with big, solemn eyes. Then the boy took a couple of shy steps forward. "Are you Zeetie's boyfriend?" he asked seriously.

"Oh, Lord," Pazit groaned. "Brian . . ."

"No," Billy said, equally serious. "I'm her friend-friend."

"Oh," said the boy and seemed to think about that. "Well, Mommy said I should ask if Zeetie's boyfriend wanted to stay and eat supper with us."

"Oh, Lord," Pazit said again.

"Tell your mommy thank you, but I have to go home and eat supper with my own family."

Brian ran back into the house, to report to his mother, Billy supposed. At least Pazit didn't look like a ghost anymore—she had turned bright pink.

"This is *so* embarrassing," Pazit said. "Believe me, I never said you were my boyfriend." And then she added, "I actually don't believe in stuff like that."

"You don't?" He was surprised. He'd never known a girl who said she didn't believe in boyfriends. He was a little disappointed, too. Maybe more than a little. Maybe a lot more.

"No," Pazit said. "It's much better just to be friends, don't you think?"

"I guess so," Billy muttered. *Maybe she's right,* he thought, and wondered what it would be like to be "just friends" with Tanya. Today he'd heard that Tanya was going to the after-the-game party tomorrow night with Jerry Winslow, the football star. *Fine,* Billy thought. If that's what Tanya wanted, she was welcome to it, even though there was a part of him that missed her. Or maybe, he thought, he just missed having a girlfriend.

"So," Pazit was saying, "what do you think I ought to do about my surprise package? I mean, what would *you* do? Tell Mr. Dalrymple about it?"

"Don't worry," Billy said and stood up. "I'll think of something. Right now I have to go home."

Tripper leaped up and followed Billy to the tree where his bike was propped. Billy bent down and scratched the dog's ears while Pazit snagged him by the collar. "Good boy," he said to the dog. "I'll call you later," he told Pazit. *"Shalom aleichem."*

Pazit grinned, an almost happy smile. *"Shalom aleichem."*

Billy wished he didn't have to go home and deal with Brenda and her bad-mouthing and with his parents, who seemed so hurt and mystified by everything that was happening. His parents didn't seem to understand anything about him. It was as though a few days ago he had a family and everyone got along pretty well, and then something happened and now they were all strangers. A few days ago he had a bunch of friends and a girlfriend, too. A few days ago he was running for student council and had a good chance of getting elected. Everything was great. And now nobody was talking to him, or if they did it was to say something nasty. Everybody was at everybody else's throats.

Billy had ridden three blocks when he had an idea. He turned around and raced back to Pazit's. "Can I borrow the package?" Billy asked when she answered the doorbell.

"Why?"

"To show some people who don't really understand what's going on."

"You want the whole thing? Contents, too?"

"Yeah. Also," he added, "if you could let me have the note they sent you about Tripper, I'd like to have that, too. See, I think if I take all that evidence and show people what's been happening to you, it's better than if you do it. I'm going to show it to my parents. Maybe that will work better than if you show it to yours."

Pazit hesitated. "OK," she said finally. "I'll be right back."

Billy waited anxiously in the living room while Pazit dashed upstairs to get what he called "the evidence," hoping that Pazit's stepmother wouldn't come out and start questioning him. While he waited, he had time to look more closely at the clay pots around the room. Some were small and squat, others tall and narrow, but all the colors were deep earth tones. Billy edged closer to a round one with a tall, graceful neck and ran his fingers over the smooth surface.

Pazit returned with a plastic sack in which Billy could make out the sharp edges of the florist's box. "The note's in there, too," Pazit said, handing over the sack. "I hope you know what you're doing, Billy."

"Me, too."

BILLY HEADED STRAIGHT for Shawn's. Cara Stovall answered the door.

"Look who's here," she said sarcastically. Billy remembered only a few weeks ago when he used to come to see Shawn and Cara hung around and hung around, making it plain that she thought Billy Harper was the most wonderful boy imaginable. Not anymore. She glared at him, pouting. "What do you want, Billy?"

"I want to talk to Shawn."

"I don't know if he wants to talk to *you*."

"Let him tell me that, then," Billy said, brushing past her. He took the stairs two at a time, knocked loudly, Beethoven's Fifth, and opened the door.

"Hey," Shawn said, obviously startled.

"Hey," Billy said, shutting the door. "It's Show-and-Tell time. First, I got something to show you, and then I got something to tell you." He opened the plastic sack and set the gift box in the middle of Shawn's bed. "Open that," he ordered.

Billy watched Shawn's face carefully as Shawn gingerly lifted the lid and peered inside. "Geez," Shawn said, making a face. "This is gross, man," he said. "What's it about?"

Billy handed him the gift card that had arrived with the box. " 'From Your Friends in the Band,' " Shawn read and then looked at the tag that said, "To Pazit."

"Well," Shawn said reluctantly, "I guess a lot of people are ticked at her."

"I guess so," Billy agreed. "Now read this." He unfolded the note printed on yellow lined paper and handed it over. Shawn read it silently as Billy watched.

Shawn sighed and handed back the note.

"That's Cara's printing, obviously."

Shawn nodded, saying nothing.

"Did you know about the note?"

"I knew Cara had sent her a note. I didn't know what it said."

"Cara threatened her. She threatened to do something to her dog. Did you know about the dead rat? Pazit saw the car, by the way. Whoever delivered the package was in Twig's car."

"I knew about it," Shawn admitted. "It wasn't

my idea, and I didn't do it, but I knew about it. Hey, listen, Billy, sometimes you have to get tough, you know what I mean? Because this girl has really screwed things up for us. For *all* of us, and that includes you, too, you know. One person has screwed things up for ninety-five other people, more than that if you count the flag team and the Demonettes. That isn't fair. She didn't ask, she didn't say anything, she just went and did it. And in a democracy you don't do that."

"This is your idea of democracy?" Billy asked. "Sending threatening notes and dead rats?"

"She's interfering with our freedom of speech," Shawn insisted, "and our freedom of religion."

"And what about hers? Have you thought of that?"

Shawn shook his head. "Maybe we better just agree to disagree," he said. "Nobody's going to win this one."

"OK," Billy said, angrily snatching up the box and the note and cramming them back in the plastic sack. "You're right. Sometimes you just have to get tough. You have to play hardball, like my dad says. So here's the deal: you and your sister and Twig and Ashleigh and everybody else who's had anything at all to do with this whole mess go to Pazit and apologize. She won't march tomorrow, but you all agree to work with her so she can march with us in the competition in October."

"You're threatening me?" Shawn laughed, a short, angry bark. "And what if we don't do it?"

"You'll find out," Billy said. "Tomorrow night."

Solo

"IT'S ENTIRELY UP to you, *mi hijita*," Gus said. "If you decide not to march with the band, that's fine. But if you decide you do want to march, that's fine, too. We back you one hundred percent no matter what you decide."

"I'm not going to march tonight," Pazit said. "But I'll play up in the stands. I know the music, after all."

"Pazit, why don't you just *quit?*" Ellen asked. "Get out of that crazy band. All it does is cause you grief."

"Because I need the P.E. credit," Pazit replied morosely, although of course it was much more than that.

"But there must be other groups at that high school where you'd fit in better than you do with that bunch and still get P.E. credit."

"What I really want is figure skating," Pazit said.

"Lots of luck," Ellen said. "Isn't there a modern dance group, for instance? I'll bet you'd enjoy that. And maybe you could do something like the school newspaper, just for fun."

The truth was, she wasn't interested in joining any group at that school. She'd never fit in, because they'd never let her. Not after what had happened. They'd always see her as the outsider, the misfit, the troublemaker, the foreigner.

Ellen talked as if it mattered, as if anything was possible now, which it obviously wasn't. *All I have to do,* Pazit thought, *is show them the note threatening Tripper and the box with the dead rat.* That would put an end to all these suggestions about how she could fit in and become a regular member of society at Jericho High School. Because the same kids who wrote the note and wrapped up the rat were the kids who worked on the paper and performed with the modern dance club. You couldn't escape it. That's just the way it was here in Jericho. But she didn't want to deal with her parents' reaction, at least not now.

"I don't think she should just lie down and be

walked over," Gus said. "She shouldn't let herself be hounded out of the band because she's made herself unpopular by bringing up a legal, constitutional issue."

"I'm not suggesting that she give up, Gus," Ellen argued. "But I also don't think it's necessary for her to be a martyr."

Pazit left them arguing and went upstairs to put on her band uniform, the white pants Ellen had helped her shorten and the red jacket with the brass buttons and rows of gold braid and gold-fringed epaulets. She set the white shako with the red plume squarely on her head and marched downstairs. Her father, who was reading a story to the boys before news time, sat up straight and saluted. The little guys, wide-eyed at her costume, imitated their dad, Matt saluting left-handed.

"Could somebody drive me over?" Pazit asked. "I have to be at the field by six, and it's too hot to walk in this uniform."

"I'll take you, since you're apparently determined to do this," Ellen said and went to find her wallet and keys.

Fifteen minutes later as they pulled up by the gate to the athletic field, Ellen asked, "Where do you think we should sit?"

Pazit's mouth fell open. "You're coming?"

"Well, yes, I thought we'd all come and watch

for a while. At least through halftime. Neither your dad nor I is much of a football fan, but we do want to see what the band is all about. And I think Matt and Brian will like the marching stuff. Especially with their big sister in it."

"I hadn't expected you to come," she said. "You don't have to."

Ellen leaned over and gave her a hug. "We'll be there, Pazit. Look for us."

Pazit grabbed her shako and her flute and climbed out. Other parents were also dropping off band kids, and Pazit quickly lost herself in the crowd. She went along with them to the band section by the ten-yard line. The manager had distributed plastic seat cushions along the aluminum bleachers, each cushion numbered to correspond to the player's marching position. Darla Jean saw Pazit assembling her flute and frowned. "You still gonna play?"

"Uh-huh," Pazit murmured.

"You sure are stubborn, I'll say that."

In the section next to the band where the Boosters usually sat, a TV crew was setting up. This time the reporter was a woman with blond hair that fell in deep ripples past her shoulders. "Hi," said the reporter, climbing back and forth over the metal bleachers and holding out a microphone to whomever she could reach, "I'm Claudia Kendall from Channel Six. How do you think it'll go this evening? Expecting any problems?"

A group clustered around her, dying to be interviewed, but Mr. Dalrymple blew two shrill blasts on his whistle, and the players reluctantly returned to their seats.

"Band!"

"Sir!"

Mr. Dalrymple gave them a pep talk about doing their best and not letting themselves be distracted, reminded them about certain places in the music where there had been problems. "All right, band," he said, "relax, have fun, and play good music!"

The players filed out of their seats and down to the assembly area beneath the stands, trailed by the reporter and the camera crew. Pazit stayed where she was, watching them leave out of the corner of her eye.

Below her the horns bleated, tuning up. Then Chuck Johnson blew his whistle and the band stepped out onto the field and formed a solid rectangle facing the press box. Pazit rose and held her flute to her lips. "Ladies and gentlemen, the Jericho High School alma mater," boomed the P.A.

Everyone stood, solemnly holding one finger in the air while Pazit and the band played the school song, set to "Ode to Joy" from Beethoven's Ninth

Symphony. As they finished, the Demons in white pants and red jerseys jogged onto the field, and the band swung into a pep song and the Demonettes started a yell. The opponents, from some school Pazit had never heard of, went through the same ritual. Then the band filed off the field and up into the stands again. When Billy passed her he winked a tiny wink.

As Jericho won the toss and the opposing team prepared to kick off, Pazit saw Gus and Ellen and the little guys making their way through a knot of people, gazing around and trying to figure out where to sit. Pazit smiled to herself. They looked so out of place, like visiting Martians. She thought of waving, but she didn't want anyone else knowing they were her family.

She wished she'd had a chance to talk to Billy. She'd seen him this morning at band practice and told him she definitely wasn't going to march, not in the opening ceremonies, not at halftime, not at all. He'd brought back the note and the box with the dead rat. She'd planned to get rid of it today, and now she realized with a sinking feeling that the corpse was still in her locker and would be in a very bad state by Monday morning.

"I'm your friend, Pazit," Billy had said. "Just remember, I'm always your friend."

She sat near the bottom of the bleachers, below

the drummers, below the big horns that stood across the top rows and blasted out "GO JERICHO" whenever the Demons had possession of the ball. At the end of the first quarter Blainville was ahead, 14–0.

Mr. Dalrymple, perched on the elevated platform in front of the stands, called "Hats!" and the band members sat up straight, their shakos on the bench beside them. "One—two—don *hats!*" ordered Mr. Dalrymple, and on cue the entire band swept their shakos onto their heads, providing the people across the field on the visitors' side with a dramatic flash of red and white.

At the beginning of the second quarter, the director called another signal, and the band filed out of the stands again. This time Billy gave her a small thumbs-up sign so that no one else would notice. The band formed up beneath the grandstand for the halftime performance. The Demonettes, who had been sitting in the first rows of the Boosters section, rose as one and made a perfectly orchestrated exit, following the band. Tonight they were attired in new outfits, skintight gleaming red bodysuits with rows of white fringe that rippled from shoulder to ankle. Their white cowboy hats were all cocked at the same precise angle. The Junior Demonettes, in their red skirts and white shirts, stayed behind.

Once they had gone, Pazit had a clear view of Ellen and Gus and the boys. Her father appeared to be reading a book, and the boys were racing toy cars back and forth on the seats. Only Ellen seemed to be paying attention to the game. Sitting not far from them was a plump black woman who Pazit finally recognized as Mrs. Wells, unfamiliar in regular street clothes. Pazit felt a little better knowing there were at least a few people present who cared about her.

A cheer went up, and Pazit glanced at the scoreboard to see that Jericho had managed to score a touchdown in the last seconds of the second quarter. But they missed the extra point, and the score was now 14–6.

As soon as the half ended, the visitors' band, dressed in purple and gold, marched out onto the field and for the next nine minutes executed their routine. *Not bad,* Pazit thought, watching critically. But she noticed a couple of uneven spaces between the marchers and the lines weren't razor straight. Jericho could beat them easily in competition, she decided, no matter how Mr. Dalrymple tried to frighten the band into thinking otherwise. When their routine ended, the home crowd clapped politely, and then it was Jericho's turn.

With Chuck Johnson strutting at the head of the line, the Jericho High School Marching Band moved smoothly, precisely out onto the field and into the first position. The band faced the home crowd and waited for the cue from Chuck, who was waiting for *his* cue from Mr. Dalrymple. On the downbeat the band launched into "Amazing Grace," and the complex pattern began to unfold. It was good, Pazit thought, in spite of herself, marching in place in the stands and playing along with them. *Very, very good.*

As they moved into the next phase, Pazit followed the musical shift easily, almost without thought. What she was doing was nonsensical, she realized. At that moment Pazit felt lonelier than ever. She was a nonmember of a band that didn't want her—period.

They segued into the final number, Mr. Dalrymple's rewrite of a hymn now called "Tribute to Landis." The line of drums, led by Billy with his bass drum followed by Shawn with his bass drum, the snares and quads right behind them, were to move through the line of cymbals and tubas and then reverse direction and meet up with trumpets and cornets coming in at an acute angle.

But instead of reversing, Billy kept on going. He was doing everything exactly the way he was supposed to—but he was going the wrong way.

For a moment Pazit could not believe what she saw happening. She could imagine the panic on the field, Shawn calling to Billy, probably some of the others, too, when they realized how badly he was screwing up. The band was preparing now for the next move, but they were falling out of sync and couldn't seem to get it together again. But Billy kept on, oblivious, steady as a clock, marching away from the band.

Billy headed straight for the stands.

Pazit kept on playing. That was one of the rules: you kept on doing what you were supposed to, even when somebody else was messing up.

Billy marched off the field and up the concrete ramp until he was standing directly in front of Pazit. He was still pounding his drum in perfect time, a huge grin spreading across his face.

"Hey, Pazit!" he called. "Listen to my drum solo! I'm dedicating it to you!"

PART FIVE

Shalom Aleichem

Dear Billy

Dear Billy,

Here I am, back in Denver for the Jewish holidays. That means, in case you didn't know (and I bet you didn't!), that I'm celebrating Rosh Hashanah, the Jewish New Year. It started Wednesday at sundown. That was the fun part. The hard part is next week, Yom Kippur, the Day of Atonement. It's a day of complete fasting that starts next Friday at sundown, and I won't be able to have anything—not even water!—until sundown Saturday. I did it last year for the first time. It's hard, but when you're with other Jews, it's not so bad.

So I can't tell you when I'm coming back, or even right now IF I'm coming back. Because it's so different being here than it was being there. Mom and I are trying to get along better, and so far it's working. (Of course, I've only been here since Tuesday!) I miss Dad a lot, and Ellen, too, and my little brothers. I got really close to them. Ellen tries so hard, and Dad is a very unusual individual, which I think you would get to appreciate if you were around him more. And, of course, I miss Tripper!

I know this sounds strange, but I love them, they're my family, but they're not Jewish. There are no Jews in Jericho! I didn't know how hard that was until I got there. I never thought about being in a place where there were *no* Jews before. It wasn't just that people were rude and insulting and insensitive (except YOU), because people can be rude and insulting and insensitive in Denver, too. But they were being that way at least partly because I'm Jewish, and to tell you the truth, I'm really sick and tired of putting up with that.

When I first moved to Jericho last summer I promised Mom and Dad and Ellen that I'd stick it out through the school year, no matter what, but none of us knew ahead of time what that meant. I can't tell you how good it was to be here for the religious holiday, which always means new clothes (not that I care about that) and delicious food (you'd love it—everything sweet like apples dipped in honey, for the new year), but maybe because you go to church and are pretty religious you have some idea what I mean. I can't explain how much I'm looking forward to this evening when it's just Mom and me and a couple of friends for the Sabbath. When Mom lights the candles and says the prayers, just the way we used to do it every Friday, I'll know I'm really home again.

So we're talking about me staying here and not going back to Jericho. Right now we're just talking, and of course I'd have to promise all kinds of things, like how I'm going to be a good student and practice my flute and clean

303

my room, and you know me! But it might actually be worth it. I'd come back to visit Dad and Ellen over the winter holiday (I refuse to call it 'Christmas holiday' for obvious reasons!) and pack up the rest of my stuff. And I'd want to see you. But you're the only person I want to see there. You and Mrs. Wells.

I will never forget a week ago tonight when you marched off the field and played your drum solo for me. That was maybe the only good thing, definitely the only *wonderful* thing that ever happened to me in Jericho. That, and your helping me build the doghouse. I wish you'd come and visit me here in Denver sometime, if I decide to stay.

Your forever friend,
Pazit

Dear Pazit

Dear Pazit,
There you are in Denver, and here I am in
Manasseh. Where's that, you ask? It's
sixty miles west of Jericho, the town my
mother's from. My aunt Myrna teaches at
Manasseh Christian School here, and I'm
enrolled as a student and living with
her and my uncle. I know what you're
thinking, and you're right!

After you left, things fell apart for
me, as you can imagine. Now I know firsthand what you were up against the whole

time you were here, everybody whispering about you, calling you names,
threatening you. And I didn't help much,
at least not in the beginning (and not in
the end, either!). So I was the next
target, only I got a double-dose because
I'm not an ''outsider,'' like you. I'm
an insider, and that makes me a traitor. My mom even got the idea that I
was possessed by the Devil, and she took
me to our pastor and asked if there was
something that could be done to get
the Devil out of me! That was just for
starters.

So, I plea-bargained. I agreed to
transfer to Manasseh Christian, where
there is no football team, no band, no
dances, but lots and lots of Bible
study. They were willing to take me after the start of school, since it was
still early in the semester. I can go
home on weekends (it's only an hour's
drive from here) but so far I haven't,
since my family's still upset with me,
and as for friends—well, you can figure
that one out.

The only good thing is, they made me

a second semester junior, so I'll graduate a year from December. Then I'm going to work for my uncle until I can get into the navy. So maybe I'll get to see the world, just like I said I wanted to, remember?

I'm still glad I did what I did, Pazit. I never felt better in my life than I did the night I marched away from the band and played that drum solo for you. I guess I had two reasons for doing it: One, I thought it was about time somebody stood up for you and took your part. The other, as I guess you know by now, is that I really do love you a lot. I think you're the bravest person I ever knew. (And also the prettiest girl in Jericho.)

I wonder if you'll decide to go back to Jericho or to stay in Denver with your mom. That's a tough one. But if and when you do come back, part of the ''plea bargain'' was that I promised my parents I wouldn't see you anymore. I'll keep that promise as long as I'm here in Manasseh, but after that, when I'm on my own, watch out! You're too special to let disappear forever. Write when you can; I didn't make any promises about letters.

Love, from your biggest admirer,
Billy